MURDER ON THE MENU

An Al Pennyback
mystery

CHARLES RAY

North Potomac, MD

For information about this and other works of this author, contact the author at charlesray.author@yahoo.com.

Cover design by the author

Cover photograph by Averie Woodard

Printed in the United States of America.

ISBN: 0692796525
ISBN-13: 978-0692796528

ONE

"Al, you put that down this instance, you hear me?"

I was just reaching for the twist-off cap on a bottle of *dos Equis* beer. I froze with my hands hovering over the bottle, my fingers twitching, and then, I slowly looked around.

Alma Mayweather, wife of my best friend, Metro DC Police Detective Buster Mayweather, stood at the top of the steps leading down from my back porch with left hand on her hip and her right hand, index finger warningly raised, pointing down at two bundles of energy playing in the scraggly grass. I looked around to see if anyone else had noticed the guilty look on my face, and thankfully, everyone's attention was on little Albert Mayweather and his twin sister, Sandra.

I took a deep breath, removed the cap with a

couple of quick twists, and took a long swallow, then took another quick look to make sure Alma wasn't looking my way, and wiped my mouth with the back of my hand. She had been talking to little Albert, my three-year-old namesake, who was holding a twelve-inch twig aloft, about to bring it down on his sister's head, but if she'd seen me use my hand rather than a napkin to wipe my mouth, her wrath could very easily have encompassed me as well.

That's right, Alma, even though she's only five-three, is not someone you trifle with. Just ask Buster, six-one, two-thirty, a former college football player, and one of the most feared cops on the DC police force, and when Alma spears him with her laser glare, he quakes in his size twelve shoes. I'm about his height and fifteen pounds lighter, so you know damn well I'm afraid of her too. She makes those Asian tiger moms look like little pussy cats.

Even little Al knew that when his mother spoke with *that* tone of voice, you listened. He sheepishly let the twig fall from his hand and stood there looking up at her with those big, brown eyes, and an innocent smile on his chubby brown face, like one of those Japanese cartoon kids. Innocent, though, he definitely was not. He was, already at the age of three, a master manipulator, able to twist everyone around his finger; everyone, that is, except his twin sister, Sandra, named for Sandra Winter, my significant other and housemate. Sandra and I, by the way, were godparents of these two often bickering bundles of joy.

Little Al, thankfully with only my first name, because *my* mother, who was enamored of the German scientist Einstein named me—you guessed it—Albert Einstein Pennyback. Unlike Albert Mayweather, who was able to use his natural charm on people, I, growing up as I did in a small town in East Texas where people were named Billy Joe, Charles Lee, or Roscoe, I had to learn to fight at an early age. But, I digress. As little Al advanced toward his mommy, who was now beaming down at her firstborn—he popped out three minutes ahead of his sister—Sandra, herself no slouch in the 'turn on the charm' department, retrieved the twig—more of a small branch about a quarter inch thick—that he'd dropped, did an amazing imitation of Jacky Robinson, and smashed it into his shoulders. It sent him flying to the bottom of the steps, caused Alma to raise her hands to her face in alarm and swoop down to scoop him into her arms as she glared at her daughter, who stood there with an innocent 'what's wrong' look on her cherubic face.

The wail that came from Al as his mother cradled him against her ample bosom, caused everyone, yours truly included, to rush toward him, except Buster, who'd been tending the grill while I got myself another beer, who dropped the spatula and dashed toward little Sandra, his face twisted into the snarl he usually reserved for gangbangers.

"Sandra," he bellowed. "You drop that stick

right now, you hear. You know you're not supposed to be hitting your brother."

The child's eyes went wide as she saw her behemoth of a dad rapidly approaching, and she let out a little squeal. Her brother stopped crying and twisted around to see what had frightened her, took in his father's angry expression, and pulled away from his mother and ran to stand between Buster and little Sandra.

"No, dada," he said, holding up his pudgy little hand like a traffic stop. "I'm not hurt."

Buster came to a jerky halt, looking down at his children, his expression a combination of anger, wonder, and amusement. Alma stood on the bottom of the steps, her gaze going from her twins to her husband, a slightly exasperated look on her face. The Dynamic Duo had struck again.

Albert and Sandra Mayweather, it seemed, were determined to turn both of their parents gray before they reached fifty. Like most siblings, they quarreled and fought, but whenever one was threatened by *anyone* else, and that included mom and dad, they came together like a Special Forces A Team, back to back against all odds.

I could tell from Buster's expression that, though this was frustrating at times, he was proud of the way they looked out for each other.

It was a lot like the relationship he and I had; in fact, it aptly described the intricate web of relationships of everyone gathered in my backyard on this sunny Saturday afternoon in July. We'd celebrated the Fourth of July with a barbecue at Buster's place on Friday, and since my birthday was coming up soon—I was approaching the big 5-3—Sandra and I decided to host everyone at our place; even after several years of living together it felt strange to think of the old farmhouse off River Road west of Potomac, Maryland as *our* place, but there you have it. She'd rented out her little house in Takoma Park, in DC, just off Georgia Avenue, and a bit south of the Montgomery County line, and moved everything she valued into my— our—place.

I'd told everyone not to bring gifts, just appetites, so of course they'd ignored me.

Buster and Alma brought a huge bowl of Alma's famous potato salad, a large German chocolate cake with my name and '53' on it in white cream, and a case of *dos Equis*, which by 2:15 in the afternoon we'd already nearly depleted; Heather Bunche, my partner at the little two-person PI agency we have off Fourth Street in Southwest DC near the waterfront, brought a large beer stein with the words, 'World's Best Boss,' in big black letters, which got a big laugh since everyone present knew that even before I made her a full partner, it had been her who kept the place going; Quincy Chang, an old army buddy who is a partner at the law firm that has on retainer, brought an expensive bottle of Merry Vale Napa Cabernet Sauvignon; and Carlton Raine, a retired CIA official, and his live-in girlfriend Elizabeth Sung brought a bushel of fresh corn that he'd raised in a little garden behind the fortified log cabin he owns in a patch of forest way west off River Road. We were saving the cabernet and cake for after dinner, the potato salad was sitting in the middle of the big wooden picnic table Sandra had picked up at Best Buy, and ten ears of corn were roasting nicely on the grill next to the hamburger patties and hotdogs.

I took another long swallow from the bottle, pulled four more from the cooler on the porch and hopped down to join Buster, Quincy and Carlton at the grill. Now that peace had been restored in the Mayweather clan, little Al and Sandra were playing a game of tag on the grassy area near the old barn under the watchful eye of the four women, who were also engaged in an animated conversation.

"Hey," I said. "Thought you guys would like something to wet your throats."

I passed the beers around. After they'd opened them, Buster, now back on grill duty, raised his bottle. "Here's to the old man," he said.

"Who are you calling old?" Carlton said, glaring at Buster. "I get I can still handle a young whippersnapper like you with one arm tied behind my back."

Buster gulped and held his hands up in mock surrender. "Uh, come on, Blood, I wasn't talking about you. I was toasting old Al here."

Carlton laughed, and winked at me. "I

know," he said. "I just like yanking your chain."

Carlton, a native of Georgia who was one of the early black men hired as a field agent by the CIA, had earned the nickname, 'Blood,' because many of his early missions had involved the spilling of copious quantities of that substance. He would never, of course, talk about them, but all you had to do was look at his steely gaze, or hear the flint in his cultured southern accent to know that this was someone you didn't screw around with. And, if that wasn't enough, one visit to his cabin, with its fortified door, the surveillance equipment in the room behind the living room, and the arsenal of weapons he kept there, would convince you that despite being over eighty, he could probably kill you without blinking or working up a sweat. Buster's one of the toughest cops on the force, having worked street gangs and homicide, but next to Alma, the only person I've ever seen intimidate him was Carlton Raine.

"Aw, I knew that," Buster said. But, there wasn't much conviction in his voice.

"Scc, thc problcm with you youngsters these days," Carlton said. "Is that you're so politically correct, you don't get a joke unless it's someone slipping on a banana peel."

"Not even that," Quincy said. "Laughing at someone's misfortune can get you in a lot of trouble in most places."

"True that." Buster shook his head as he flipped the burgers, now nice and brown on one side. "Even when you got a perp in cuffs, you gotta be careful what you say to 'em, or even within earshot. One wrong word and the ombudsman's all over you like flies on dead meat."

Carlton chuckled. "Of course, the good old days weren't all that good either. In a way, the political correctness is probably best. Back in my younger days, people could be really spiteful with some of the things they said."

I could only imagine what he must have gone through. I'd joined the army right out of high school, during the closing days of the Vietnam War, and while it had been a pioneer in equal opportunity, for men at least, there were still a lot of people who judged you by your melanin count rather than your rank.

"Anyway," Carlton said, lifting his bottle. "I'd like to second young Buster's toast. Happy birthday, *young* man; welcome to what just might be the most interesting phase of your life."

We clinked bottles and drank. Wrapped in the warmth of their friendship, getting older didn't seem so bad. Quincy and I made the next beer cooler run, and we were near the bottom of those bottles by the time the burger patties were brown, the franks were beginning to curl at the ends, and the cord was giving off a sweet aroma that made my mouth water.

"Okay, everyone, get some plates, this meat's as ready as it'll ever be," Buster yelled.

The kids immediately forgot their game of tag and raced to stand in front of their father, with hungry expressions on their cherubic faces. In that they were every bit their father's children; never late for a meal and never turn down seconds. Buster looked down at them, his medium brown face alight with pride.

"You two get up there on the porch where your momma's set up for you," he said in a gentle voice. "I'll fix your plates. What would you like, hamburgers or hotdogs?"

"Both," they said in unison.

Like I said, they're truly Buster's kids.

"Okay, get on up on the porch, and I'll bring you one burger and one hotdog."

"I want corn and potato salad, too," little Al said.

"Me too, me too," echoed little Sandra.

"No problem, you'll get some of everything."

He constructed two burgers and two hotdogs, adding a small amount of catchup and mustard, and a burger and a dog each on two paper plates, to which he also added an ear of corn. He took that up to the porch, where Alma added some of her potato salad, and Sandra ladled on a little mound of baked beans that she'd whipped up.

While the kids were attacking their food, the women got eight plates—the ceramic kind—and brought them to the grill, where I helped Buster make burgers and hotdogs for everyone. The plates were put on the picnic table, the men on one side, the women on the other, and everyone began helping themselves to corn, potato salad and beans.

"Who wants a beer?" I asked. Everyone but Alma and Sandra raised a hand, so I went to the cooler and got six bottles which I took back to the table. "What about you Alma, what would you like? I know Sandra wants white wine."

"White wine sounds fine to me."

"Me too," Heather said, pushing her beer away.

"Me three," Elizabeth said.

"Well, jeez, you could have told me that before I lugged that beer out here," I said.

"You didn't say you had white wine," Heather said. "Besides, you guys will drink the beer anyway, so you're actually saving a trip."

I couldn't argue with that, so I trotted to the kitchen. I retrieved a bottle of Molino A Vento Pinot Grigio from the fridge and removed the cork. I then got four wine glasses from the cabinet over the fridge and put glasses and wine on a large round tray and took them back outside.

"Shall I pour, ladies?" I asked.

"No, we can pour for ourselves," Sandra said, taking the bottle from the tray with one hand, while passing the glasses around with the other. "You sit and eat."

I didn't need a second invitation to do that. The smell of grilled meat and corn was causing my mouth to water and my stomach was rumbling. I walked around and sat on the end of the built-in bench, next to Buster and across from Sandra.

For the next ten minutes the only

conversation was 'pass the potato salad,' 'more beans,' and 'this corn is so sweet,' interspersed among the crunching sound of teeth gnawing the sweet kernels off the cob, and the occasional lip smack or sigh of contentment.

The guys had a head start on me, but it didn't take me long to catch up, and Buster and I finished our first serving at about the same time. We looked at each other.

"You up for seconds?" I asked.

"Does a bear do it in the woods? Damn straight I am, birthday boy."

"Buster Mayweather, you watch your language," Alma said in a raspy voice that was meant to be a whisper. "Remember, little pitchers have big ears."

"Oops, sorry mama, it just slipped out." He looked at me again. "They repeat everything they hear, man, and I mean *everything*."

We were both laughing as we went back to get our second set of burgers, hotdogs and corn. Back at the table, I debated for a full ten seconds whether or not to pass on the potato salad and beans, thought to hell with it, you only have one birthday a year, and helped myself to a generous amount of both.

Shortly afterwards, Quincy and Carlton got up to get seconds. The women were still, not exactly dawdling, but eating a lot slower than we were.

When Quincy and Carlton came back, Buster rapped the tabletop with the hilt of his knife.

"Could I have your attention please?"

Everyone stopped eating and all eyes focused on him. He lifted his beer; I thought he was about to propose a toast, but instead, he took a drink.

"Buster Mayweather, will you stop messing around and say what you got to say." Alma tried for a stern tone, but there was a twinkle in her eye. The two of them were up to something, and I had an itchy feeling it had to do with me.

I like puzzles, live for solving them, but I'm no fan of surprises. I can be spontaneous, to a degree, but I appreciate a bit of predictability.

I could feel a tightening in my gut.

Now, I know that sounds weird. After all, I'm not just a private eye who has gone up against some pretty rough characters, I'm a combat vet, with dozens of pretty dicey special operations missions under my belt, some in places that, if I told you the names, I'd have to kill you—just kidding, sort of—and in combat, the only thing that's predictable is that everything will be unpredictable, but in my everyday life, I like things to be . . . predictable.

Buster milked the silence for a few more beats, until Alma made a snorting sound through her nose.

"Okay, okay," he said. "Here's the deal, guys. I got this friend from college, Bob Campbell. He lives in upstate New York, up near Lake Erie. He played a few years in the NFL, but last year he blew out his knee and decided to call it quits." He paused and took another sip of beer.

"Anyway, he went back home, and decided to use the money he saved while he was playing pro ball to open a restaurant. It's gonna be one of them fusion places, you know, different foods from around the world. He's got his grand opening next week, and he wants us to come up for it, and he's picking up the tab. All we gotta do is buy the gas to drive up and back."

"Hey, man, that's great," I said, slapping him on the back. "You taking the kids?"

"Well, yeah, but it's better'n that, bro. You're invited too."

I almost choked on the mouthful of hotdog I'd just swallowed. "Me? Why?

"Because, bro, it's your birthday, and because you and Sandra haven't had a vacation in a long time, and because my buddy's willing to pay the full boat." He looked around the table. "And, everyone around this table's invited."

Charles Ray

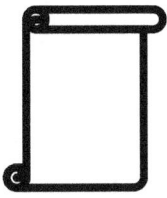

TWO

Buster's little announcement got everyone around the table talking at once. For a few seconds it sounded like a crowd pressing in around the last table of sales items at a Macy's bargain basement sale. Even the kids, who had finished their food and, too full to get up to mischief, had been playing quietly on the porch, came down to see what the fuss was about.

"Come on folks," Buster said in the voice he usually reserved for telling perps to hit the bricks face down. "I can't understand you when you all talk at once."

We stopped talking.

I took advantage of my position as host, well, technically co-host, to speak first. Of course, I raised my hand to signal my intent to do so.

"That's an awful nice gesture," I said. "But, this guy's your friend. I can see him inviting you and your family." I looked around the table and did a quick headcount. "But, the six of us make one helluva plus one. You sure your friend's up with that?"

Buster gave me a look that was so cold I almost shivered. He didn't have to say anything, because the look said it all—I'd just insulted him. Of course, he wouldn't have made such an offer without clearing it first.

"Bro, I'm hurt," he said. "I already talked to Bob about this, and he said it's cool."

"But, so many people would cost a lot of money," Sandra said.

"Did I mention he owns a small hotel? Right on this lake, kind of a resort, with fishing and sailing and everything. Believe me, this dude can afford it. In addition to the money he made in the NFL, he had family money."

I looked at Sandra. Her dark blue eyes looked back at me, a placid expression on her face. Sandra and I have been an item for nearly a decade. I met her when I was investigating the murder of one of her students at Carver High School, the inner city school where she teaches language arts. After a rocky start, we hit it off, and pretty quickly discovered that we were a good fit. We've made no real commitment, at least not verbally, but it's sort of understood that we're in an exclusive relationship. I'm not one for throwing the 'L' word around lightly, but deep down inside where it counts, I love her and she loves me, and we know it without having to say it. Likewise, even with the placid expression on her face, I knew she really wanted to accept this invitation.

Of course, I had the other woman in my life to think about. Heather came to work for me as an assistant when I first opened A.E. Pennyback, Confidential Enquiries, and with her ability to coax information from the ether via her computer or from the many people she has in her address book, she quickly became the indispensable member of the firm. I made her partner a couple years back, and now she has a PI license in Maryland, the District, and Virginia just like me. She's a natural blonde like Sandra, but totally unlike her in almost everything else. Sandra's tall, 5-11, and athletic, with lots of wiry muscle under her shapely curves, while Heather's short, 5-2 in heels, and while she knows a few karate moves, is not what you call athletic. Sandra teaches kids at one of the toughest schools in DC, loves her kids, and is great with people. Heather, while good on the phone wheedling information out of people, prefers interacting through the computer. Unmarried, and not in a relationship, the company is pretty much her life. She's at her desk every morning at 8:00 when I arrive, and unless I shoo her out, is still there around 5:00 when I bag it for the day. I couldn't just bail, even for only a few days, without checking it with her first.

"I don't know if we can spare the time from work," I said.

"We don't have any cases right now," Heather said. She looked across at Quincy, who would be the source of most of our cases.

"Nothing from Holcombe, Stein and Chang," he said. "In fact, I'm kind of thinking that I could use a few days off myself."

One of the advantages, I guess, of being a senior partner, and the source of most of the firm's billable hours. That was the trump card, though. Quincy and I go all the way back to my days as a young lieutenant colonel in command of a special operations team at Ft. Bragg, North Carolina, and he was an army lawyer in the Judge Advocate General's Office at post headquarters. He left the army for private practice a few years before I checked out after my wife and son were killed in an auto accident sending me into a downward spiral from which I might not have recovered but for him suggesting I become a private investigator and then arranging for his firm to put me on a ten thousand buck a month retainer.

"Well," I said. "I suppose I could take a few days off."

"In fact, we could just lock the place up for a few days and both take the time off," Heather said.

Now, that really did it for me. I owed Sandra a vacation, and Quincy didn't see any immediate work on the horizon, but, when workaholic Heather is up for taking time off, it's time to pack the sunscreen and get a neighbor to pick up your mail.

"Okay, count us in," I said to Buster. Sandra rewarded me with s big smile, and a promise in her eyes of further rewards when we were alone.

"Me too," Heather said.

"Count me in," Quincy said.

"Hm, while it sounds like a fascinating offer," Carlton said. "I'm afraid that Elizabeth and I will have to pass."

"Yes," she said. "We're going to Georgia to visit some of Carlton's relatives that he hasn't seen in a long time."

A look passed between them, just a brief glimmer that I almost missed, but I saw pain in Carlton's brown eyes, and a look of concern in Elizabeth's. But, it passed quickly, and the two of them looked back at me with placid expressions, expressions that were as phony as three dollar bills. Something was going on. But, this was neither the time nor place to pursue it, so I shoved it into one of the back rooms of my brain with a note attached, 'Find out what's up with Blood.'

Buster, though, was too elated with the responses he'd gotten to notice. "That's great," he said. "I'll call Bob right away and tell him to expect six grownups and two bratty little kids. He's gonna be over the moon when he hears this."

"This guy must really be loaded to be excited at the prospect of having to pay the expenses for eight people," I said.

Buster laughed. "Well, he ain't exactly poor, you dig, but it's not that. Bob was an only child, and so were his mom and pop. So, when they died a few years back, that left him without any close family. That's what we're gonna be at this restaurant opening; the family he never had."

Put that way, I felt bad that I'd even

hesitated about going. I was an only child myself, and my parents had been swept away in a hurricane a few years after I disappointed my mom by joining the army instead of packing off to college like she'd always envisioned me doing.

"In that case, amigo, I'm honored to accept the invitation." I looked at Sandra, who returned my gaze with a knowing smile. "I think this is gonna be a great vacation."

"Yeah, it'll be nice not to have to worry about tracking deadbeat clients or dodging bad guys," Heather said.

"Just peace and quiet," I said, nodding my agreement.

THREE

Sandra and I got up early Sunday, and after a run through the forest and a workout on the heavy bag in the barn, we did a light breakfast, packed—me for three days, and her enough, I thought, for three weeks—and loaded our bags into the backseat of my bright green Volkswagen, and at 10:30, started out.

Buster had written directions to the little town of Lakeview, located on the northeast shore of Lake Chautauqua, about 15 miles south of Lake Erie. He'd given us two possible routes; one, via the Pennsylvania Turnpike to I-90 near Erie, Pennsylvania and then northeast into New York, to New York State Road 394 which would take us south to the town of Mayville, where we would turn east and follow a county road around the northern end of the lake until we came to Lakeview; the other took us north on I-70 through Hagerstown, Maryland, and into Pennsylvania until we got to

US 219 north, with a bunch of diversions until we entered Allegheny National Forest in the south and emerged at the town of Warren in the north, from which US 62 to Jamestown, New York, at the southern end of Lake Chautauqua, and followed the eastern shore of the lake to Lakeview. The turnpike was the easiest route, but the one through the national forest looked more interesting, and certainly more scenic, so by mutual consent, Sandra and I decided to take that one. We'd made arrangements to meet up with the Mayweathers, Quincy, and Heather when we arrived. They, of course, were taking the less scenic route, and Heather, when we told her the route we planned to take, cautioned me not to 'get lost.' As if. I've navigated my way through trackless deserts and triple canopy jungles, sometimes with bad guys shooting at me; there was no way in hell I'd miss a big damn lake that if I just kept driving north I'd eventually drive into.

Sunday morning traffic on River Road was light, but as usual, the I-495 Beltway was bumper to bumper from the River Road exit to the I-270 interchange, and I got more than a few angry blares of horns and middle fingers as I made my way from the far right lane to the left two lanes to get off the Beltway to the main north-south route up through the eastern part of western Maryland into central Pennsylvania. Northbound traffic on I-270 was moderate from the interchange to Germantown, bit heavy from there to Frederick, and light from Frederick to I-70. There's not much to see on 270 until you get north of Germantown and hit farm country. Once you leave Montgomery County, the views to both sides until you hit places like Frederick and Hagerstown are scenic forests, farms, and pastureland. Once on I-70, and northwest of Hagerstown, it's pretty much all farmland, and this major east-west Interstate connecting Baltimore, Maryland to cities in the Midwest, is not as heavily traveled as the I-95 north-south corridor, especially on Sunday.

Once we left the interstate highway system near Schellsburg and started driving north, it was like we'd been transported back in time. Except for Altoona, which is a moderately large industrial town, the towns we passed through, with their steepled churches, clapboard houses, and on-street parking, looked like Norman Rockwell paintings.

I'd listened to the local NPR station's Sunday morning classical music program until we got out of range. I tried surfing the channels—surfing is a word I learned from Heather, who used it to describe trolling for information on the Internet, but aptly described what I did with my car radio when I traveled—but to my dismay, I kept getting local talk shows, religions programs, and country music, so I gave up and shut the radio off.

Sandra had been quiet since our trip started, just staring out the window at the passing scenery, so when she spoke, I flinched.

"You should try around 80 or 90 megahertz," she said. "Outside the Washington area, that's where most of the public broadcast stations are."

Where she learned that, I do not know, but I twisted the dial until it was on 80 and turned the radio back on. All I got was the raspy sound of static. She reached over and turned, and damn if we didn't hit an NPR station playing big band music from the thirties and forties at 88.9.

"Where'd you pick up that little piece of information?" I asked.

"One of the teachers at Carter is an NPR fan, and she visits her family in Pittsburgh every summer. For some reason she shared that little factoid with me in the school cafeteria one day at lunch. I never thought I'd ever need to know something like that, but it just goes to show, you can never know too much "

I smiled and tapped my fingers on the steering wheel to the sound of Tommy Dorsey's orchestra playing 'On the Sunny Side of the Street.' Sandra smiled, and turned her attention back to the idyllic looking farmland through which we were driving.

At 1:15, we were entering the outskirts of the little town of Westover, about half our journey finished. My stomach started growling.

"Hey, babe," I said. "I'm feeling a little hungry. You wanta stop here for something to eat?"

"I'm hungry, too. What'll it be, Burger King

or Taco Bell?"

There wasn't a lot of enthusiasm in her voice. I'm something of a fast food junkie, especially when I'm busy or traveling. She, on the other hand, prefers eating food that's minimally processed and possessed of less than a full day's recommended amount of calories, which, unfortunately, can't be said about most of the fast food offerings along our highways and byways.

"Let's see if there's a mom and pop place serving local fare," I said.

She gave me a raised-eyebrow look?

"Really? What is local fare, by the way?"

I had my eyes on the road, but realizing that she'd asked the question in all seriousness, I darted a quick glance her way. I realized that other than crab and other seafood on the Chesapeake shores, cheesesteak sandwiches in Philadelphia, and bagels in New York, I had no idea what people north of the District ate. Given the English, German and Dutch influences of the western areas of Pennsylvania and New York, I figured whatever it was would be heavy on potatoes and sausage.

"That, my dear, is a good question. Do you feel adventurous?"

She smiled at me. "Why not? It can't be any more dangerous than the fat- and carbohydrate-laden stuff you get in the drive-through joints."

Yeah, I thought, but will it taste as good. I am well aware that fast food, and most processed and prepackaged food, for that matter, are laden with salt, sugar, and fat to hook people on them without providing much in the way of nutritional value, but dammit, my taste buds needed their daily fix of those three ingredients as much as a junkie needs his heroin fix.

As we got well into the little town, another Rockwell-like village with a real-life town square that we had to navigate around, a barber shop complete with a red and white striped pole next to the door, I also saw the ubiquitous yellow arches and other signs of the no-waiting because it's precooked and kept hot in a microwave food joints, some familiar, some not; approximately two in each block. A lot of eateries for a town that looked like it had a population that would be straining to top ten thousand. Just as I was about to give up on anything but fast food, I saw the little gray brick building sitting alone in the middle of a parking lot, surrounded by pickups and mud-splattered vans, with a sign that said in crudely painted black letters,

"Hey, that looks like a local establishment," I said. "And, from the number of trucks and vans, it seems to be quite popular."

She looked at the place, her brow wrinkled. She didn't have to say anything; I knew she was thinking that maybe a fast food place might not be so bad.

"Come on," I said. "Where's your sense of adventure."

"Okay, but if I get food poison, I'm not cleaning up the vomit." She shuddered, and shrank down in her seat as I pulled into the parking lot and slipped the Volkswagen into an empty parking space not far from the front door.

I double-checked to make sure all the doors were locked after we got out. As I pushed open the scarred wooden entrance door, a heavy aroma of cooking grease hit me in the face like a cardboard panel in a high wind, and the smell of cooking grease—yes, grease, not vegetable oil—crawled up my nose, bringing back memories of the roadside barbecue stands that were common in East Texas when I was a kid, places with a tin roof on poles, no walls, super-long wooden picnic tables, and a big, brick fire pit in the back on which a side of beef or an entire pig would be roasting from sunup until it was nothing but picked bones.

As the parking lot indicated, the place was busy. There were twenty tables, each with four chairs, and only two of them were unoccupied. There was a bar in back, facing the door, behind which stood a man about six-seven and at least three hundred pounds, wearing a white apron around his huge waist and a white cap on a head the size of a small pumpkin. He was serving drinks, draft beer mostly, to four men in overalls and John Deere caps who had plates piled high with dark brown meat and mashed potatoes. They alternated between shoveling food into their mouths and washing it down with beer. There were a few couples, but most of the diners were men, dressed similarly to the men at the bar, except for three or four men in dark suits, all of them accompanied by women in colorful dresses; probably couples stopping for lunch after church. A few heads raised and turned our way when we entered, and were just as quickly turned away. The sight of a six-foot, dark brown-skinned man dressed in brown chino pants and a blue polo shirt with a five-eleven, blonde amazon dressed similarly hanging onto his arm was either something they were accustomed to, or strange, but they were too shocked or polite to stare.

Sandra's grip on my forearm tightened as we stepped farther into the place. It took a few seconds for my eyes to adjust to the difference in light. Outside, with few clouds in the sky, it had been bright, but the dust and grease on the windows, and the low wattage bulbs in the overhead fixtures, caused the interior of Al's Eats to look like the early hours of dusk. With the door closed behind us, the smell of food cooking was even stronger, but not too unpleasant. I have a fondness for fried food, and my nose was telling me that much of the fare here was fried.

The fat man behind the bar, unlike his customers, kept his eyes on us as we approached. He didn't look particularly hostile, but he also didn't look particularly welcoming.

He just appraised us, me mostly, with small dark eyes that seemed like little pebbles of coal in the folds of flesh that made up his face.

"Just the two of you?" he asked as we reached the bar.

"Yeah," I replied. "Just the two of us."

He reached under the bar. I tensed. He brought out to plastic-covered sheets of paper and handed them across the bar.

"We have everything that's on the menu," he said. "Take any empty table, and I'll be right over to take your order."

I took the menus, and we turned toward the empty tables, which were near the bar.

"Hey, Al, kin I git another beer?" one of the men at the bar called out.

"Yeah, comin' up," the fat bartender said in the same tone of voice he'd used with me.

I let out a breath I hadn't even realized I'd been holding. It wasn't me. The fat man spoke that way to everyone. I guess that's just northern hospitality. We reached the table, and I pulled out a chair and held it for Sandra, then took one opposite her where I had a view of the door and a good bit of the room. The bar was behind me about six feet, but the way the place was laid out, I couldn't watch the bar *and* the door, so I settled for watching the door. I handed her one of the laminated menus.

"The meat loaf and mashed potatoes looks good," she said after studying it for a few minutes.

"I was thinking about the fried chicken

dinner, myself," I said.

"Good choices," Al, the fat bartender said from right at my left elbow. *Damn*, for such a big man he moved quietly. "Would you like iced tea with that, or lemonade?"

"Lemonade," Sandra said. She smiled up at him as she handed him her menu. His cheeks darkened and he smiled back.

"Same for me," I said. He was still smiling when he took my menu.

"Food'll be ready in a few minutes. I'll git your drinks now."

He turned and, surprisingly agile for such a fat man, went back behind the bar, where he busied himself putting ice and a yellowish liquid into two large glasses, which he brought back to us. Then he went back behind the bar, and through a door into what I assumed was the kitchen.

"Interesting place," Sandra said. She took a sip of lemonade, and smiled. "Hm, good."

I sipped my lemonade. It was good. A combination of sweet tartness, or tart sweetness, that set up a buzz in my mouth. I looked at my glass. I saw a seed floating in it. My estimation of Al's place went up a notch. Most places serve lemonade made from a powder, but this was fresh-squeezed and with just enough sugar—this guy had run a lemonade stand in his childhood that was for sure.

"It sure is," I agreed.

He was also true to his word about the food.

We hadn't even taken our second sips when it arrived. Fresh looking, steam still rising off the surface, but plates not too hot, which meant they hadn't been zapped in a microwave, and in more than generous proportions. He put a plate loaded with three pieces of golden brown fried chicken, two drumsticks and a thigh, a half cob of roast corn, sweet peas, and a square of cornbread in front of me, and a fist-sized chunk of meat loaf with a mountain of creamy mashed potatoes with brown gravy flowing down its sides like lava in front of Sandra.

"Enjoy," he said, and went back behind the bar.

Enjoy we did. The bill came to less than twenty dollars. I gave him a twenty and a five, which caused him to smile for the second time since we'd walked in.

"The food was great," Sandra said.

He blushed again, and his smile got wider. "Why, thank you, little lady. You be sure'n tell your friends about Al's, and you two have a safe trip."

"Maybe we'll stop here on our way back," I said.

"You do that," he said like he really meant it.

Maybe, I thought, there's something called northern hospitality after all.

Charles Ray

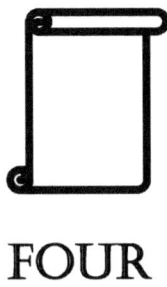

FOUR

The rest of the trip was pretty uneventful. Traffic through the Allegheny National Forest was light, and except for a few places where the trees were sparse enough that you could see beyond them, the forest grew so close to the highway, all you could see was trees, trees, and more trees.

We left the national forest at Warren, Pennsylvania, got on US 62 north, and drove through several more small towns. If there was a 'Welcome to New York' sign, I missed it. I only became aware that we were no longer in Pennsylvania when I saw a sign for a real estate agency that billed itself as 'The Top-selling Real Estate Agency in Upstate New York,' complete with an address in Jamestown, New York. I figured a New York agency wouldn't be advertising in Pennsylvania, and sure enough, soon after that I began seeing road markers for New York state roads and Chautauqua County roads.

I looked at my watch. It was 4:00 pm, and we were less than thirty miles from our destination. Even with the stop for lunch, we'd made good time.

In New York, approaching Lake Erie, the land flattened out into rolling farmland, and little towns tucked into low-lying hills. The architecture was similar to central Pennsylvania; lots of wood frame houses with wide front porches, tidy lawns, many with detached garages, and white picket fences; or small farms with red barns and silver silos, and cows or horses grazing lazily in lush green pastures.

We approached Lake Chautauqua from the southeast, driving through Jamestown, the county seat of Chautauqua County, known, according to a sign on the outskirts, as the home of Lucille Ball, the redheaded comedian I remember watching as a kid. It wasn't much different from any of the other towns we'd passed through, other than being slightly larger, and having, of course, county government buildings.

The drive north, with the lake to our left, was interesting, but nothing to write home about. In some places, the lake shore was undeveloped, but only in a very few. Houses and boat docks on our left, and houses with boat trailers in the driveway on the right, was what we had to look at until we were just outside the town of Lakeview, where to our right were rows of grape vines and fruit trees, and to our left a green strip of neatly cut grass led downward to a brownish gray strip of beach. From here, we could see the lake, with several sailboats zipping across its placid blue surface, and the shore beyond with docks and little lakeside inns nestled in groves of stately trees.

Lakeview itself was called a township, which was, I suppose, meant to confer some kind of status. It was what the old folks where I grew up in East Texas called a 'stop in the road.'

The highway, State Road 430, became the main street, appropriately named, Main Street, a two-lane thoroughfare with parking lanes on both sides. Two gas stations stood at the entrance to town, facing each other across Main Street. Next to them were the obligatory fast food places, McDonald's with its golden arches on the right and a Sonic on the left. The rest of the town was given over to more or less traditional business fare, a barber shop, a Pik 'n Save grocery shop, a CVS drug store with a Post Office sign and logo in the window, an antique store, a hardware store, and an art gallery made up the bulk of what I assume the locals called 'downtown,' with a garage and auto supply store and a Dollar Giant facing off against each other at the north end of Main Street. That was the town. It didn't even have a traffic light, just a sign right before the gas stations warning that the speed limit was 35, down from the 45 it had been.

As we neared the north end of town, I looked

for Rose Street on the left, which, according to Buster's instructions, led to a lakeside resort development containing the Allegheny Resort and Spa, where our host had booked accommodations for us, a sailing school and marina, a restaurant called Rizzoli's, and our host's soon-to-open, Fantastic Fusions Restaurant, and next to that a Dollar Giant only slightly smaller than the one in town, but with more cars in its parking lot. In fact, we'd seen few people on the sidewalks when we drive through Lakeview, but here in the resort, we saw dozens of people, singles, couples, and families, some dressed in the rough and ready garb of working people and some in the bizarre, bright print shorts and shorts of people on vacation. It looked as if the resort was slowly bleeding the town of its customer base.

The hotel was surrounded by a large macadam parking lot that looked half full, mostly expensive late model cars along with a few vans and campers. The drive through the parking lot curved up under a white stone canopy. A young guy wearing black pants and a short, red jacket stood on the curb. When we pulled to a stop in front of the glass double doors of the main entrance, he waved, and another young man wearing the same uniform, emerged through the double doors and rushed to the passenger side of my Volkswagen. He opened the door and offered a hand to assist Sandra's exit.

"Welcome to the Allegheny Resort and Spa,"

he said. "Do you have reservations?"

I got out of the car. "Yes, Mr. Pennyback and Ms. Winter," I said over the top of the car. "The reservations were made by Robert Campbell."

"Ah, you're Mr. Campbell's guests. You're the last to arrive. The others have already checked in. If you'll give me your car keys, I'll take care of getting your luggage to your room, and Brad here will park your car."

Wow; first class service. I could get used to this kind of treatment. "Thanks er—"

"I'm Kevin," he said. "I'm the senior bell manager."

I walked around the front of the car and handed Brad my keys. "Thanks, Kevin. We don't have too much luggage, as you can see. It's all in the back seat."

He'd already opened the rear door and was hefting our bags out and stacking them gently and neatly on the curb. "No problem," he said without looking back at me. "You can go ahead to the front desk and get your keys. I'll have your things in before you finish signing the register."

I was blown away the moment I walked through the silently swinging double doors. The lobby was huge. It seemed to stretch forever toward the back of the building, an impression enhanced by the fact that floor and walls were an off-white marble, or close enough to marble to fool me. The reception desk looked to be made of the same material, but with gold filigree around the top.

Three people stood behind the desk, a man and two women. The women looked like young Stepford Wives, complete with lacquered hair, shiny skin, and pasted on smiles. The man also had lacquered hair, shiny skin, and a pasted on smile, but the skin of his face didn't move when he smiled, making him look like an exhibit from Madame Toussaint's Wax Museum. We headed for the Stepford Wife on the left. Her smile got broader.

"Good afternoon," she said. "Welcome to Allegheny Resort and Spa. Do you have a reservation?"

I started to go through the same spiel. She interrupted me as soon as I got to Campbell's name.

"Of course. Ms. Winter and Mr. Pennyback; we have you booked in the honeymoon suite on the mezzanine level." She swiveled a leather-bound book around, opened it and put a gold Mont Blanc pen, the kind that cost nearly three hundred bucks each, on it, and shoved it toward me. "If you'd please just sign on the top line, you can sign for the both of you. I'll have the bellman bring your bags up immediately. If there's anything we can do to make your stay more pleasant, I'm Shari, that's with an 'I,' please don't hesitate to call me."

It sounded like a well-researched speech. It was impressive in its delivery, though. I was adding the tips up in my head. Campbell might be picking up the tab for the room and board, but with service like this, Sandra would insist on generous tips for the staff. The weekend was gonna cost me a couple hundred at least, but as I looked around at all the marble, expensive furniture, and understated, but expensive-looking decorations, I decided it would be worth it.

If the lobby impressed me, our suite knocked me for a loop. The walls were a repeat of the lobby motif, but the floor covered in a plush deep purple carpet, which I would normally have considered a bit of garish overstatement, but somehow, here, it worked. The furniture in the suite's living room was French provincial; medium brown wood covered with violet upholstery containing gold highlights. Reproductions of art prints, landscapes and street scenes, were tastefully arranged on the walls facing the large windows which gave a view of the lake. The bedroom repeated the pattern, with a king-sized bed in the center of the floor. The beige silk bed spread was covered with deep red rose petals. Again, a large window gave a view of the lake. Even the bathroom, with a shower large enough for a volleyball team, and a large step-in tub with massaging jets, was impressive, all white marble with gold inlaid around the baseboards and golden fixtures in the beige marble basin, toilet, bidet, shower, and tub. If the Sheik of Araby came back, he would insist on such accommodations for his harem.

The bellman who'd taken our luggage arrived just as we reentered the living room. He insisted on putting them in the large walk-in closet, and informed us that a maid would come and turn down our bed at 6:00, an hour hence, giving me a knowing look as his glance shifted toward the large bed. I tipped him five bucks. He was still smiling that 'I know what you're planning' smile when he left.

I looked at Sandra and then at the bed. She looked at the bed, smiled, and started unbuttoning her blouse.

Just as I reached for the top button of my shirt, a melodic chime echoed throughout the room.

"Damn," Sandra said. "Someone's at the door."

"I guess it wouldn't do to ignore them, would it?"

She fastened the two buttons she'd undone, and headed for the door. A few seconds later she returned holding a small square envelope.

"It was the bellboy with a message from the front desk," she said. "Along with their apologies for neglecting to give it to us when we checked in." She held it out to me.

"You go ahead and open it," I said.

"What if it's a private message for you?"

"Who up here would be sending me private messages?"

She shrugged. "Good point." She opened the envelope and withdrew a folded piece of paper. After opening it, she squinted for a few seconds at it and then laughed. "It's a note from Buster." She handed it to me.

Buster's handwriting is about as crabby and hard to read as a doctor's prescription,

Al/Sandra
If we don't see
you guys in the lobby
Meet us at the pool.
Buster

I refolded the note and tossed it onto the dresser top. "Well, I guess we'll have to test this bed later, babe. You fancy a dip in the hotel pool?"

Charles Ray

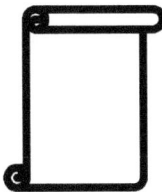

FIVE

I don't look too bad in swim trunks. I've got a little extra weight around the middle, but at 53, that's to be expected; my metabolism is slower, so I have to work twice as hard to burn the calories, and more of what I eat wants to settle as comfortable fat, especially around the belly. But, I can still look down and see my feet without bending forward, and I don't have to search for my willy when I take a pee. So what if I don't turn heads when I stroll on the beach.

Sandra, on the other hand, hasn't an ounce of superfluous flesh on her tall, smooth, curvy, athletic body. Even in a one-piece blue bathing suit that covered the mound of her butt instead of letting the bottom half hang out, and without a hint of breast showing at the side; but with a tantalizing bit of cleavage in front; even the women lounging poolside, stopped reading their fashion magazines and tracked her as we walked past. The guys were just short of letting their tongues hang out.

We walked past about ten people lounging around the pool; there was only one swimmer, a slim-muscled type who was gliding along just below the surface with smooth strokes that I envied.

Buster, Alma, and the twins were at the kiddie pool in a fenced-in area behind the pool proper. Buster, his eyes closed, was draped over a folding beach chair that sagged under his weight, and Alma was kneeling at the edge of the pool watching the twins splash each other. She turned her head at the creaking of the gate when we entered the kiddie pool area.

"All right, you two, be careful," she said to the twins as she rose and came over and hugged Sandra. She gave me a smile. "Girl, don't you look good in that outfit. I wish I had your body."

This was high praise coming from a woman who, despite being short, had curves in all the right places, and her dark brown flawless skin was prominently displayed by the modest yellow bikini she wore.

"That's for sure," Buster said. His eyes were no longer closed. He looked from Sandra to Alma. "But, you don't look too bad yourself, mama."

Now, that was a quick recovery, not that it wasn't true and, from the look in his eyes as he gazed up at his wife, completely sincere. Alma put he her hands on her hip and did a little gyration that I'm sure sent every male pulse in the vicinity, except mine, racing. I do not covet my best friend's wife, not even in my mind, because if I did, Buster would mangle me, and Sandra would finish the job—case closed.

"They both look good," I said. "All you gotta do is see all the goggling eyes back there by the pool."

Buster sat up and glared across the fence. "Long as goggling is all they do," he said. "Ebony and Ivory here are already spoken for."

"More like caramel and vanilla, because we're so sweet," Alma said, thrusting her ample breasts in his direction.

"As always, you're right." He threw up his hands in mock surrender.

"Smart man," I said.

He smiled up at me. "How was the trip? We were beginning to worry about you two."

He patted the empty lounger next to him. I sat, gingerly, because the metal frame, even that late in the day, was still quite warm. Once I was settled, I filled him in in on our trip. His eyes lit up when I got to the part about Al's Eats.

"You mean they got a white version of Mom's way the hell up here?"

"Yeah; it's not exactly soul food; well, I guess it's what white folks think of as soul food, but man, it was scrumptious."

"And you were the only person of . . . the

nonwhite persuasion in the place?"

I laughed. "The only thing darker than me was the meat loaf. But, I didn't get any negative vibes. Just a bunch of working class stiffs enjoying Sunday dinner."

"Dang, man; sounds like your trip was a whole lot more interesting than mine. The only interesting scenery was the tunnel, and that's only 'cause the kids thought it was neat driving into the ground like that, and the food . . . well, if I never have another fast food burger it'll be too soon, know what I mean."

We compared total driving times, and it turned out that the turnpike route was longer by over fifty miles and wasn't even faster despite higher speed limits on the interstates. They made it in about five and a half hours as compared to our shade over six.

"That does it," Buster said. "We're following you guys on the trip back. Say, whaddya think of this place, classy ain't it?"

"Classy hardly begins to describe this place. Driving here, through all the small towns and farm country, this is the last thing I expected to see. From the parking lot and the pool here, I guess there's no shortage of paying customers."

"Yeah, that's what Bob says. This place makes pretty good money. He's just starting the restaurant 'cause he said he's always wanted to own one."

"Whoa, you telling me your friend owns this hotel too?"

"Sure, but he inherited it from his dad . . .

well, technically from his mom, I guess, but he always wanted to own something he started all by himself, that's why the restaurant."

"So, the money he made in the NFL's not why he's able to start a restaurant, one of the riskiest businesses to go into?"

"Uh, no, I guess not," Buster said. "But, if I know Bob, that's the money he's using. He was that way in college, too; wouldn't ever take money from his folks even though they were filthy rich. He worked or used student loans to get his degree, and then paid off his student loans after he started in the NFL."

I'd never laid eyes on this Bob Campbell, but I was already beginning to like him, and I said as much to Buster.

"Well," he said. "Now you get to meet him in the flesh."

A shadow fell over me. I turned and looked up. A broad shouldered silhouette was blocking the sun.

Charles Ray

SIX

Robert Campbell looked like a former football player; not the image I had of an independently wealthy man who could comp four total strangers in his hotel, and certainly not a man who owned a place as ritzy as the Allegheny.

The blue blazer he wore strained to contain his shoulders, and his hands were as big as softballs. He was a little thick around the waist, but, he looked fit. His nose was slightly bent, probably from a break that wasn't set properly. He was as tall as Buster, and about the same weight. His light brown hair was cut close on the sides and medium length on top. He smiled broadly.

"Hey, Bruiser, long time no see," he said in a booming voice. "Howya been?"

Buster bounded off the lounger and the

two hugged each other, and then did a complicated hand slap and fist bump.

"What up, Wreckin' Ball? I been copasetic," Buster said. "Got myself two kids now." He pointed at the kiddie pool.

Alma and Sandra walked over. Buster put his arms around Alma's shoulder. "This is Alma, my sweet cakes," he said. "The Amazon's Sandra Winter, she's with the tall drink of water here. Meet my good buddy, Al Pennyback."

I stood and stuck out a hand. The guy had a strong grip, but he wasn't one of those macho meatheads who tried to crush your hand to prove how strong he was.

"Nice to meet you, Mr. Pennyback, you too Ms. Winter," he said.

"Just call me Al," I said.

"And, I'm must Sandra," she said, walking over and standing next to me.

"And, I'm Alma," Alma said. She wriggled out of Buster's embrace and walked over to stand in front of Campbell, her hands on her hips. "Why did you call my husband Bruiser, and why did he call you Wrecking Ball?"

Campbell looked at Buster and raised an eyebrow. "You never told her?"

"Naw, it never come up." He shrugged.

Alma stamped a foot, a useless gesture since she was barefoot and the surface around the kiddie pool was some kind of foam material. I put a hand over my mouth to keep from laughing. Buster tried, but a little huff of laughter escaped before he got his mouth completely covered. She stamped her foot again, and spun, raising a finger at him.

"Don't you be laughing at me, Buster Mayweather." She turned back to Campbell. "Are you going to tell me about your . . . nicknames?"

Campbell laughed. "I must say, I'm not surprised that Buster fell for you," he said. "You're a real firecracker." She frowned and made a growling noise. He held his hands up, palms out. "Okay, I'll tell you, tonight at supper. I'd like to meet the rest of Bruiser, er, Buster's friends, so how's about I wait and tell everyone?"

Alma scrunched her eyes close for a couple of seconds. "Okay, I'll accept that."

"By the way," Campbell said. "There were supposed to be two more people, where are they?"

"We're right here," Heather said, as she and Quincy approached the gate.

They were dressed for the pool; Quincy wore a pair of baggy swim trunks that hung precariously on his frame, and Heather wore a blue bikini that didn't cover much. I noticed Campbell's eyebrows climb, and his eyes widen as he looked at her.

"Ah, you must be Heather Bunche," he said, shoving a hand at her. "You're as beautiful as Buster said." He gave her hand a shake and held on a few seconds longer than was absolutely necessary. She smiled up at him, that thousand watt smile of hers that she reserves for special people. Campbell finally released her hand and turned to Quincy. "And I presume that you sir, are Quincy Chang, Esquire, one of the most feared barristers in our nation's capital."

"You presume correctly," Quincy said, taking his hand. "And, you are Robert 'Wrecking Ball' Campbell. You were one of my favorite defensive backs . . . no, strike that, you *are* one of my favorites."

"Well, it's always nice to meet a fan." He turned to me. "What about you, Al, you look like you played a little football in your day? Are you a fan?"

"I played in high school, but that was over thirty years ago.'

"Wow, you don't look that old. How do you stay in such good shape?"

"Well, I exercise a lot."

Buster slapped my shoulder. "Don't let him blow smoke at you, bro," he said. "Al here was a Green Beret. This dude knows more ways to kill you with his bare hands than you can count. You know, he refuses to even pack heat."

"That's right; Buster said you were a private detective. That must be interesting work."

"Mostly just checking records and going through files," I said.

"Which is what *I* do," Heather said. "While, Al here runs around the streets whipping the bad guys."

Campbell's jaw dropped. He turned and looked at Heather with eyes like saucers. "*You* work for a private investigator?"

"She *is* a PI," I said.

"Well, well, tonight's dinner conversation will be interesting," he said. "You must tell me all about your work."

Heather was beaming. I hadn't seen her look at a guy like she looked at Campbell for a long time, and the way he was looking at her, I could tell that he was impressed with more than the way she filled out her bikini.

"By the way, where are we eating dinner?" Buster asked.

"Why, here in the spa, of course."

"I thought we'd be eating in your new restaurant."

"Oh no, we're saving that for tomorrow night at the official opening. Vivienne, that's Vivienne LeClerc, my head chef, wants to make sure the kitchen's pristine for the opening tomorrow, and that the inaugural dishes are served after the ribbon's cut. She's not allowing anyone, and I mean anyone, in that kitchen except herself and Walter Muncie, the sous chef."

Buster shot a look at Alma. "Man, this Vivienne sounds like a real dragon lady."

"*Oui*, it is true that I am sometimes *la dame dragon*," a sultry voice with a strong French accent said from behind me. "But, it is only to ensure that the restaurant opening is perfect. *Est-ce pas ce que tu désires, Robert?*"

"Of course it's what I want, Vivienne," Campbell said. "Folks, meet Mademoiselle Vivienne LeClerc, head chef of Fantastic Fusions, and Walter Muncie, her sous chef."

We all turned to get a look at the new arrival, two new arrivals in fact. Vivienne LeClerc couldn't have been a millimeter over five feet tall, but she was perfectly proportioned, with clear creamy skin, dark brown hair pulled back in a severe bun, and sparkling brown eyes so dark they looked black. She had what's known as a whiskey voice, deep and husky, and she looked her listener straight in the eye when she spoke. The three-quarter length sleeve white over-blouse and black pants she wore clung lovingly to every curve of her body. The only flaw in her otherwise perfect appearance was the flat, canvas-sole shoes she wore. Behind her stood a tall, stoop-shouldered kid who looked to be in his late teens, with a narrow face, buck teeth, reddish brown hair that flopped over his brow, and a bad case of acne. His long-sleeved white jacket and black trousers hung on his frame. His canvas-sole shoes, though, looked like they were pinching feet whose size were out of proportion to the body they supported.

"*Je me réjouis de vous rencontrer vous, Mesdames et Messieurs,*" she said. "I hope that you will enjoy the menu tomorrow.

Walter and I have worked very hard to make everything perfect, is that not right, Walter?"

Muncie swallowed; his Adam's apple bobbing up and down. A flicker of a frown creased his face, quickly replaced by a stiff smile.

"Yeah, we've been working our ass—, our backsides off to make everything perfect."

Campbell put an arm around the small woman's shoulder, and smiled at Muncie. "I know you guys have been going at it, and I appreciate your efforts. That's why I think you need to kick back and enjoy a quiet meal prepared by someone else for a change."

"But, Robert," LeClerc said with a trace of annoyance in her voice. "If you are to show Gavin Laine that his objections to Fantastic Fusions are wrong, we do not have the luxury to, as you say, kick back."

"Who's Gavin Laine?" I asked.

Campbell looked annoyed. "Gavin's the owner of Rizzoli's Restaurant," he said. "You might say he's something of a thorn in my side.'

"*Alors!* That is the understatement. The man has been trying to prevent us from opening the restaurant. I think he is the one responsible for the sabotage."

My trouble antenna went up. "Sabotage?"

Campbell glared at LeClerc. "We don't know that it's sabotage, Vivienne," he said. "It could just be a series of unfortunate accidents." To me he said, "There've been a few mishaps in the building; water left running, an infestation of roaches, and the like. They threatened to delay our opening, but we got them fixed."

"No thanks to your friend, *Monsieur* Laine." LeClerc's voice carried a haughtiness that can only be conveyed with a French accent.

"Let it drop, Vivienne," Campbell said. "Everything's back on track now for tomorrow's opening. There's no sense dwelling on the past. Tonight let's just enjoy our dinner."

She smiled up at him, and linked her arm through his, which brought a boyish smile to his face.

"As you wish, *mon cher,*" she said. "But, I cannot stay late at dinner. I still have some preparations to make for tomorrow."

"Must you work so hard?" Campbell frowned.

"If we are to have a successful opening, and a successful business, we must do the hard work in advance, *mon cher,* that is the only way. Walter and I must make a few last minute preparations, but when they are done, I assure you, you will appreciate it."

Campbell tried frowning, but his lips refused to cooperate, and he ended up smiling. "Very well," he said. "I can never win an argument with you, can I?"

They reminded me of Buster and Alma. Despite her diminutive size, Vivienne LeClerc was the alpha in the relationship just as Alma was dominant in her relationship with Buster, and like Buster, Robert Campbell not only accepted it, he seemed to like it.

Out of the corner of my eye, though, I noticed that Walter Muncie did not look like a happy camper.

Charles Ray

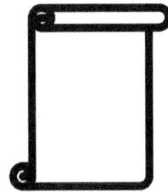

SEVEN

Campbell, LeClerc and Muncie left us to go to the spa's dining room to set up for our dinner. The rest of us retired to our respective rooms to change clothes. Campbell had insisted that the twins also be included in the dinner invitation, telling Alma that he would make 'special' arrangements for them.

With an hour to spare, Sandra and I christened the bed appropriately, scattering rose petals all over the place, before showering and donning our evening attire. I opted for a blue shirt, dark blue pants, and a light blue jacket, while Sandra was decked out in a figure-hugging dress that stopped tantalizingly at mid-thigh, and displayed an ample amount of cleavage. Neither of us ordinarily went for such displays, but this was a special occasion, and we were being entertained by a genuine tycoon, so it seemed called for.

We decided to take the stairs from the mezzanine level down to the first floor restaurant rather than the elevator, and I wasn't kidding myself, I went along with it because it gave me a chance to show my lady off to the other guys in the hotel, all of them giving me jealous glances as we slowly descended the curving stairs to the lobby. Not a few women took a long look as well; I wasn't sure if they were looking at me or envying Sandra, but I puffed my chest out anyway, because both scenarios were nice to contemplate.

The restaurant was in the rear of the lobby directly opposite the main entrance. We entered it through a large marble archway. A waiter dressed in black pants and a white jacket with gold piping, a Fernando Lamas look-alike, met us at the entrance. He made a small bow.

"*Senor y senorita*, please allow me to show you to your table," he said. He even had the old actor's gravelly voice.

"How do you know which table is ours?" I asked.

"You are Senor Campbell's guests, Senor Pennyback and Senorita Winter, are you not?" I nodded. "Senor Campbell, Senorita LeClerc, and Senor Muncie are already here. I will show you the way."

He turned and walked toward the right rear of the expansive room. We made our way among dozens of tables covered in snowy white linen, set with expensive-looking silverware and other accouterments. Even the salt and pepper shakers looked like they cost more than I made in a week of hard work.

Our host and his staff sat at a large circular table that was separated from the main dining room by a large blue silk screen. Campbell had changed into a dark blue blazer over gray pants and a beige shirt, making me glad I'd chosen as I did. LeClerc wore white pants, still hugging her every curve, and a long-sleeved white jacket. Her hair was still in a bun, and as she stood and walked around the table to greet us, I saw that she was still wearing the sensible flat, canvas-soled shoes. Muncie looked as if he hadn't bothered to change his clothes or comb his hair.

"Al, Sandra," Campbell said. "You're the first to arrive. What would you like to drink? No, wait, let me guess. Sandra, I think you're a white wine drinker. I have a sauvignon blanc that I think you'll love, and Al, I peg you as a . . . beer drinker . . . I just got a shipment of Hasenbrau in from Munich. I assume you like German beer?"

Now, there's not a beer drinker on the planet who doesn't prefer German beers over all others, and Hasenbrau, or Rabbit Beer, is one of the most famous Bavarian beers, at least among travelers who've been to the famous Oktoberfest in Munich it is.

"Love it," I said. "I'm surprised that you don't import your wine from Germany, too. I'm no wine drinker, but their Riesling isn't half bad."

"Pah!" LeClerc said as she lightly embraced Sandra and gave her an air kiss in the vicinity of her right cheek. "The Germans make a good beer, but only in France do we know how to make *real* wine. As the *chef de restaurant*, I would not allow German wine to be served with my food."

Oops, I thought, I put my foot in it on that one. I'd forgotten about the animosity that Germans and French have for each other; always simmering just below the surface, and nothing can bring it out like hinting that Germany can make wine as good as France. Campbell saw my discomfort, and damn if he didn't seem to be quietly enjoying it.

"Of course, Mademoiselle LeClerc, everyone knows that France makes the best wines." Except the Australians, the South Africans, the Chileans, every vineyard in Napa Valley, and, yes, the Germans, but you don't insult the cook who is preparing your food. "I simply meant that since Mr. Campbell is importing beer from Germany, I assumed he would import wine as well."

She pursed her lips and blew a puff of air through them. "You are forgiven, but only if you call me Vivienne," she said. "You are, after all, American, and everyone knows that Americans have no real understanding of the world beyond our shores."

Ouch! That was a low blow—not far from the truth, but a low blow nonetheless. Then I noticed that she was smiling impishly, and I realized that I'd just been had.

"*Touche*, Vivienne, you got me there."

Campbell smiled and rolled his eyes.

"I can see that you two are gonna get along just fine." He raised his hand and snapped his fingers. "Bennie," he called to the Fernando Lamas look-alike. "Could we order drinks?"

The man hurried over. "Si, *Senor* Campbell. What would you like?"

"A white wine, the sauvignon blanc, please, and two Hasenbraus, if you please."

"Make that *two* white wines," LeClerc said, holding up her empty glass.

The looks she got from Campbell and Muncie told me the empty wasn't her first. She looked steady enough at a glance, but looking closer, I could see that her eyes were a bit bloodshot and a bit bleary looking, but it wasn't my problem. If Campbell was saying nothing, there was nothing for me to say.

"*Si, senorita*, one white wine for the lady," the waiter said. With a wry look at Campbell, he turned and walked toward the bar in the back.

There was a strained silence at the table

until he returned with our drinks balanced on a silver tray.

"Al, I'd like to introduce Benito Suarez," Campbell said, as the waiter placed our drinks in front of us. "He's been senior wait staff at the spa here for five years, but when we open tomorrow he'll be the *maître d'* at Fusions."

"Congratulations, Senor Suarez," I said, raising my beer.

"Please, *senor*, just call me Bennie," he said. He inclined his head in a slight bow. "My *papa* is *Senor Suarez.*"

I raised my bottle of Hasenbrau higher. "Well, congratulations, Bennie, I wish you the best, and you can just call me Al. Makes me nervous when people call me mister, no matter the language."

"*Muchas gracias,* Al. It was nice of *Senor* Campbell to hire me."

"Aw hell, Bennie," Campbell said. "You're doing me the favor by taking the job."

Suarez smiled and shrugged his shoulders, but the look in his eyes said he knew that Campbell was right.

"Anyway," Suarez said. "Please enjoy the wine and beer. I will have someone take your order as soon as the rest of your party arrives."

Without waiting for acknowledgement, he turned and walked back to stand near the entrance. It appeared that he was *maître d'* in everything but name already. I was tempted to ask Campbell how much of a raise he was giving him, but thought better of it. Sandra would verbally flay me for it when we got back to the room, and from what I'd seen of the man, I could figure he was the generous type.

"I take it your restaurant's fully staffed," I said.

"Yeah, I have Vivienne in charge of the kitchen, and in addition to Walt, she has four helpers. I'll be putting Bennie in charge of the dining room and wait staff. Right now, we have four busboys and six wait staff, three men and three women. For the back office, I have a secretary and an accountant." He held up his left hand with index and second fingers crossed. "Barring some unforeseen incident, we're ready for the opening tomorrow night."

He sounded optimistic. I'd read somewhere, though, that 60 percent of restaurants fail in the first year, and 80 percent don't make it to their fifth anniversary. Most fail because they open in bad locations, either places without an adequate flow of customers, or where rent and other costs are so high they can't make a profit. They also have a problem of competing with the rubber stamp style food of the fast food joints. People have become so jaded from burgers that taste the same no matter where you buy them, that one meal that's slightly off will turn them off an eatery quicker than you can say ptomaine, and in the age of instant communication, a bad dining experience can be a death warrant for a restaurant. Celebrities, especially sports figures, trade on their renown and hope that'll see them through. A famous name will get them in the door, but a bad meal will send them right back out.

Campbell didn't impress me as the typical pro jock, too much money and not enough brain cells to know how to manage it wisely. After working with Buster for a decade, I knew that some football players were more than just a number on a jersey. Still, I was curious as to why he would open a restaurant in a small area where there were already two; I had to count the dining room in the spa. Surely the local population wasn't big enough to support three upscale dining establishments.

"Will you have enough customers year-round to make it worthwhile?" I asked. Sandra shot me a quick warning look. I smiled and shrugged.

If Campbell was offended by my nosiness he didn't show it. "Yeah, as a matter of fact, we do," he said. "Bayview itself isn't that large, but on this side of the lake alone, there are six towns of over nine thousand people within ten miles, and with several on the west shore of the lake within thirty minutes or less driving distance, we have a customer base of over a hundred thousand. And, that's just the permanent residents. During the summer season and major holidays, we get a couple hundred thousand tourists, and the one thing they will all do at some point or other is eat. You might not have noticed, but every town you drive through has at least four fast food joints, and they all turn a profit. People up here like to eat, and we'll just be an alternative dining experience."

"Sounds like you've done your homework."

"Well, at college, I did major in business administration, and after I left the NFL, I went to Harvard and got my MBA."

Well, hell, my opinion of this guy just kept getting ratcheted up. It sounded like he had his stuff totally together. I turned my attention to my beer. Hasenbrau, a Bavarian beer, brewed mostly in the area around Munich and Augsburg, is a yeasty brew with a bit of a bite. I'd encountered it when my special ops detachment did NATO training with the Germans in Berchtesgaden. In the evenings after we'd finished, we'd sit around with our German counterparts and drink Hasenbrau and eat bratwurst and dark German bread with tangy mustard. Lowenbrau, or Lion beer, is one of Germany's main exports, and the one most Americans know. Only a true beer aficionado would know about, much less appreciate Hasenbrau.

"Hey, what you guys drinking?" Buster's deep voice echoed off the walls. He came in, trailed by Alma and the twins, Quincy and Heather. Buster was wearing a short blue jacket over jeans that showed off his musculature, while Alma and Sandra were dressed in light blue, a knee-length dress for her, matching dress for little Sandra. Albert's outfit matched his father's. Quincy wore a lightweight gray suit, pearl shirt, and blue tie, and Heather wore an off the shoulder green cocktail dress that clung to her hips and ended three inches from her knees.

Campbell, Muncie and I rose to greet them.

"Al and I are having Hasenbrau," Campbell said. "The ladies are having white wine. That okay with you guys? We can order lemonade or coke for the kids."

"Sounds fine by me," Buster said.

"I'll have white wine," Alma said.

Heather and Quincy also asked for white wine.

"I wanta Pepsi," little Albert said.

Suarez, who had guided them over, patted him on the head. "No problem, little man, a Pepsi it is, and what about you little lady?' He smiled down at Sandra. "You want a Pepsi too?"

She put her pudgy little hands on her hips and threw her head back. "No, I wanna grape Fanta," she said.

"Grape Fanta you shall have." Suarez laughed. "I'll be right back with those drinks folks, in the meantime, why don't you take a look at the menu and decide what you want to eat." He looked at Alma and then at the two chairs that had been fitted with toddler seats. "Would you like my help getting them settled, *senora*?"

"No," she said. "I got it." She picked up Al, the squirmiest of the two, and put him in one chair, and then put Sandra in the other. They began immediately to use the spoons and forks as drumsticks, beating on the table. Fortunately, Alma was seated between them, so they couldn't use each other's heads as drums.

"What's good?" Buster asked.

"Just about everything," Campbell said. "But, I recommend the ribeye special. They marinate the meat in brandy overnight. It's so tender you can cut it with a fork. It's almost as tender as genuine Kobe beef."

Everyone agreed that the ribeye sounded good. Alma worried that it steak would be too much

"Don't worry, senora," Suarez said. "Might I suggest the Little Cowboy special for the children? It's ground ribeye with vegetables; a child-sized serving. That way, they will be eating the same as you, but in a more appropriate form."

She agreed that that sounded good, and he went off to let the kitchen know what to prepare.

"Damn," Campbell muttered, looking toward the entrance.

I had to crane to see around the column holding the left side of the screen. "What's up?"

He pointed. "It's Gavin Laine, and he's headed this way."

Leaning to the side a bit more, I saw the person he was pointing at. Gavin Laine wasn't exactly fat, but his expensive charcoal gray jacket bulged a bit around the middle, no doubt the result of too many hours spent sitting behind a desk or at a dining table. His head was narrow, with sunken, sallow cheeks, and his eyes were deep set and too close together. He crossed the room with a purposeful stride, his gaze laser-focused on Campbell. His lips were curved down in a snarl.

When he was four feet from Campbell, he stopped and planted his hands, curled into fists, on his hips.

"Robert," he said.

"Gavin," Campbell responded.

"You think about what I said to you yesterday?"

"Yeah, I thought about it."

"So, what are you going to do about it?"

Campbell chuckled. "Why, I'm gonna go ahead with my restaurant opening as planned."

Under the pallor, Laine's cheeks darkened. He blinked like a man suddenly waking up in a strange room. He blew air out through his narrow nose.

"You're making a mistake, Robert. You don't know what you're getting into."

"Oh, I think I do. I'm getting into the restaurant business. I've researched it thoroughly, and I don't believe the presence of another restaurant, especially one serving an entirely different cuisine, will harm your business."

Laine opened his mouth, and then, he looked around at the rest of us as if he was just noticing that we were there. He took a deep breath.

"It's on your head, then, bucko. Don't say I didn't warn you."

He spun on his heel and walked away.

For several seconds, there was silence at our table. Even the twins stared silently at Laine's retreating back.

"What was that all about?" Buster asked.

"Sounds like I've been warned," Campbell said.

Charles Ray

EIGHT

Buster and I had agreed to get together for breakfast the following morning. Alma had left us right after dessert the night before to put the twins to bed. LeClerc, a tad unsteady on her feet after four glasses of wine, had also left early with Muncie—to take a last look at preparations for the opening—leaving Campbell, Quincy, Heather, Buster, Sandra and me to finish the two bottles of cabernet Campbell had ordered just before dessert.

Sandra pleaded a hangover when I woke her at 5:45 and begged off joining me in the spa's gym, so I got up, despite feeling like cold oatmeal myself, and worked out until 6:30. I showered and changed in the gym locker room so I wouldn't wake Sandra, and with my sweaty workout gear wrapped in one of the spa's big towels, joined Buster in the dining room at 7:00.

Despite having drunk a couple more glasses than me, and not being one to get up early to exercise, he didn't show a trace of the previous evening's debauchery, while it had taken working up a sweat in the gym to flush the sour taste of wine from my mouth and clear the cobwebs from my brain.

Buster had already loaded up two plates from the breakfast buffet line and was digging in like a man just rescued from a deserted island when I arrived.

"Hey, bro," he said around a mouthful of food. "Grab your grub and dig in." He picked up a slice of crispy bacon and stuffed it into his mouth, making short work of it and the stuff that was already there. "This ain't as good as Mom's food, but it runs a close second." He was referring to our favorite eating spot in DC, a soul food joint on Sixteenth Street where everything is fried except the dessert.

"Doesn't look like you left much," I said as I jinked left toward the line. "Try eating slower, so I don't have you watching me while I eat."

"Don't fret," he shot back at me. "I'm goin' for seconds when this is done."

Knowing Buster, he probably wasn't kidding. The man can eat as much as three people and doesn't seem to gain an ounce. Of course, he's so damn big—mostly muscle—

it'd be hard to tell if he *did* put on a little extra.

The buffet line looked good. It smelled good. And, it was stocked to the hilt; scrambled eggs all yellow and fluffy, stacks of pancakes, crispy bacon and sausage patties side by side in warming trays, fluffy biscuits, little squares of hash brown potatoes, and fried tomato slices. And, that was just the first half of the line. There were also large crystal bowls piled high with plums, apples, oranges, strawberries, and grapes; tall stacks of white and wheat bread slices next to a big toaster, the kind where you put the slice in at the top and it comes out toasted in a tray at the bottom; three pyramids of small boxes of cereal, next to which were little bowls of raisins, peanuts, pine nuts, and dried red cranberries. Next to the dry cereal was oatmeal and Cream of Wheat, in small boxes. The last third of the line had two milk dispensers, one whole milk and one low-fat, and four juice dispensers, orange, apple, grapefruit and cranberry. A few feet beyond the main buffet line, a cook, complete with white hat and apron, stood behind a large grill built into a table. The sign on the front of the table said 'Egg Station,' and a small tray filled with eggs balanced on the edge of the table. An elderly couple holding empty plates stood in front of the table watching the cook put the finishing touches on two omelets.

Say what you will about northerners, they

like eating as much as southerners do.

I went to the end of the line, picked up a plate and filled it with scrambled eggs, bacon, hash browns, and three pancakes. I got a glass of cranberry juice and took my food back to the table.

Buster had already poured me a cup of coffee from the carafe in the center of the table.

"That all you gonna eat?" he asked.

"Hey, I'm still digesting last night's steak."

He shrugged and resumed eating. The aroma of the bacon drew my attention to my own plate, so I fell to and began to demolish its contents. The more I ate, the more I wanted to eat. It was like priming a pump with water to get water. Pretty soon, my plate was almost as empty as Buster's two plates. He kept sneaking glances at me as he demolished his food. When our plates were empty, he sat back, rubbed his stomach and smiled.

"Ready for seconds?"

I couldn't resist smiling back. "Okay, let's go."

He only filled one plate, and I pretty much filled another. Back at the table, he went at his food at a slower pace, while I, my appetite stimulated, dug in like a starving man.

"I knew you were pulling my leg about not being hungry," he said. I just smiled and kept eating. "Say, what'd you think 'bout that dude Laine last night? Sounded to me like he was threatening Bob."

I'd pushed the brief encounter with Campbell's competitor to the back of my mind.

"It's a cutthroat business. He probably thinks your friend's gonna cut into his profits."

"Tough titty. It ain't no reason to be dissin' a dude in front of company, know what I mean?"

I did know what he meant, and it was clear that he was upset about it. The rough street patois only crept into his speech when he was upset, or he wanted to intimidate someone.

"Like I said, it's a cutthroat business. Besides, your friend looks like he's capable of taking care of himself. Which reminds me, last night you two promised to tell us where your nicknames came from, and you didn't deliver."

He ducked his head and put his hand over his mouth. "Shoot, I was hopin' everbody'd forgot about that."

"Well, I didn't, so spill it."

He really looked discomfited. I didn't like talking about some of the things I'd done in the military, but I'd never known an athlete who didn't like bragging about his exploits— on or off the field. He sighed.

"Oh hell, I guess it don't matter anymore. When Bob and me were playing together in college, we were like a tag team in the defensive backfield. When we hit a runner or pass catcher, chances were they'd have to take the poor dude off the field on a stretcher, or if we didn't hit him too hard, he'd have to sit out four or five plays. That's when we got the nicknames."

I didn't get it. To me it just sounded like the two of them were assets to their team and threats to the opposition. "So, you're telling me that the two of you were tough players. What's the big deal?"

"I used to brag about it, but then when I married Alma, she said it was stupid to brag about hurting people," he said. "Then, the twins come along, and I realized, I don't want them growin' up thinkin' it's okay to hurt people, you dig."

Shit, I should have figured that out myself. Buster's just about the best husband and dad I know—not that I now many. He'll do anything for his family; that much I can understand. Before I lost my family, I was the same way. In fact, I felt that way about Sandra.

"I get it, bro," I said. "I'll never bring the subject up again. You might want to tell your buddy, Bob, so he doesn't bring it up again."

"Oh, it's too late already. Little Al's taken to callin' me bwoozer instead of daddy. His sister's just like her mom, though, she thinks it's bad to 'bwooze' people."

By the time he stopped talking, using a high-pitched voice to mimic his kids, I was laughing so hard I had to hold my sides. He started to laugh, and was cut off by the ringing of his phone. He answered, and then his face turned serious, really serious.

"What's the matter, Buster?"

He broke the connection. "That was Bob; he wants us to come to the restaurant right away. He has a problem, a big problem, and he needs our help."

"What kind of a problem in a restaurant would either of us be qualified to deal with?"

"He has a corpse in his freezer."

Charles Ray

NINE

What Campbell didn't tell Buster, and what we found out after we bolted from the dining room, raced across the lobby and jogged across the parking lot to Fantastic Fusion, was that the corpse in his freezer, a large industrial size reefer in which hung several sides of beef, pork and other unidentifiable cuts of meat along with stacks of boxes of frozen foods, was none other than Vivienne LeClerc.

The freezer was about thirty feet by thirty feet with a six-foot wide aisle down the middle. LeClerc, still dressed in the garb she wore at dinner the night before, lay face down about ten feet from the big steel door, and if not for the bluish tint of her skin and the large dark bruise on the left side of her face, she could have been just sleeping off all the wine she'd consumed the night before. Campbell stood just inside the freezer, his arms wrapped around his middle, and from the stricken look on his face, not entirely from the cold. He was not alone. A short, dark skinned young man with close-cropped curly hair, a tiny Asian girl with the prominent cheekbones of a Korean, and a dour-looking Indian or Pakistani man of middle years, stood in a group just to his left. They all word pastel blue jackets and white pants.

Buster and I had come in through the open front door, through the dining area and into the kitchen. The freezer was off to the right of the gigantic kitchen.

Campbell looked relieved when he saw us. "Oh, thank God, you got here before the police."

"What the hell happened?" Buster said.

"I don't know. Sanjay here found her and called me right away." He pointed at the Indian man. "This is Sanjay Guptar, he's the head waiter."

Buster turned to the man. "What happened?"

"I do not know," Guptar said in his clipped British/Indian accent. "Jerome, Sunyi and I came in early to begin setting up for the ceremony this evening. Miss LeClerc and Mr. Muncie are usually here early as well, but when I looked in the kitchen I did not see anyone."

Buster stood in the door of the freezer and looked at the body, his head cocked to one side. He was going into full police detective mode. "Was the freezer door closed?"

"Yes, it was closed."

He wheeled around and leveled a finger at the man. "So, how'd you come to discover the body?"

Guptar shrank back from Buster's accusing finger. His eyes went wide. "As I said, Miss LeClerc is usually here, but I did not see her this morning. I needed to check and make sure we have enough ice for the opening reception, so I opened the freezer." He pointed to six large plastic bags stacked on the left side of the freezer. "When I opened the door, I saw her . . . lying there."

"Did you touch the body, or move anything?"

"Naw," the young black man said. "He just squealed like a little girl. Sunyi and me came running back and found him standing there with his hand over his mouth."

"I . . . I was startled when I saw her like that," Guptar said.

Buster switched his attention to the young man. "And, you are?"

"Jerome Collins. I'm one of the waiters."

"And, you, Miss?"

"I am Sunyi Kim," the girl said. She avoided looking at the still body in the freezer, keeping her eyes glued to a point a few inches in front of her feet.

"So, you came back and saw the body," Buster said. "What'd you do next?"

"Well," Collins said. "I had Sunyi call Mr. Campbell, and I went in and checked to see if she . . . if Ms. LeClerc . . . was still alive. I could tell, though, the minute I touched her wrist, she was dead. She's stiff as a board and cold, man she so cold."

"Did you move the body?"

"Naw, other than lifting her hand to check her pulse. Soon's I knew she was dead, I come back out here. I didn't touch anything else in there, and neither did Sanjay or Sunyi."

"Bob, did you call the police?"

"Yeah, right after I called you." His body shook like a willow tree in the wind. "They should be here any minute now. Buster, what the hell am I gonna do? What do you think happened?"

I kept an ear on what they were saying, but my eyes were taking in the scene; the body, face down on the floor, the stacks of boxes off to the right, and the bags of ice on the left, and all that meat hanging from metal racks overhead. It's a habit. Just like Buster going into cop mode in a crisis, I'm an investigator.

"That'll be for the local cops to determine," I heard Buster say.

Just then, I heard the muted 'whirp, whirp' of a police siren, accompanied by the louder sound of a fire engine or ambulance.

"Sounds like the gendarmes have arrived," I said.

And, it was with a loud sound that they arrived. Way back in the kitchen we could hear the bang of the front door being slammed open, and the thump of hard-soled shoes on the polished wooden floors of the dining area. The door to the kitchen was already open, or I imagine it too would have been shoved open with a clatter. The arrival of three men in uniform surprised me. On their way in they sounded like an entire SWAT team.

The man in charge was obvious, he had four stars on the collar of his blue uniform shirt, a swagger in his step, and a belligerent look on his florid face. He looked to be in his late forties or early fifties, and from the way his belly hung over his gun belt, in need of a few more trips to the gym and fewer trips to the dinner table. The two cops who came in behind him were younger and looked fitter; one had his blond hair in a Marine Corps buzz cut, and the other, two shades darker than Buster, had a shaved head.

"All right, where's the body?" the fat cop asked. "And, who the hell are all these people?"

Campbell pointed into the freezer. "It's in here, Chief Holiday," he said. "As for *these people*, you know my staff. These two gentlemen are friends of mine from

Washington, DC, up here for the restaurant opening. Buster, Al, this is Samuel Holiday, Lakeview's chief of police."

Holiday stepped into the door. His brow furrowed when he saw the body. He pointed at the blond cop. "Cory, go call Doctor Johnson and tell him we got a popsicle and we'll need him to come and establish cause of death. Who found the body?"

"Uh, I did," Guptar said.

"Delwood," he said to the young black cop. "You take this gentleman into the dining room and get his statement. The rest of you, please step away from the freezer, don't touch anything, and we'll get your statements as soon as we can." Turning to Campbell, he said, "Any idea what happened here?"

Looking like a man in a daze, Campbell shook his head slowly. "No, chief, Sanjay is the one who found her. Sunyi called me and I came here and . . . " His voice just trailed off.

The blond cop returned. A man and a woman, wearing dark blue coveralls with Chautauqua County Fire and Rescue patches on the sleeves and carrying bulky medical kits and a folded stretcher, followed him.

"Chief, Doc Walters will be here in about ten minutes," he said. "What do you want the EMTs to do?"

Holiday blinked. "Uh, I guess they could move the body to the ambulance. Might make it easier for the doc to examine it."

"Don't you think it would be better to

leave it where it is until you've taken photos, and had your crime scene techs examine the scene for any trace?" Buster's voice was level, but I caught the tension in it.

Holiday might be chief of police, but even I knew he was going about things in the wrong way. His face went tight. He had caught the tone in Buster's voice too, and like most stupid people he didn't like having his stupidity pointed out.

"What are you, some kind of TV cop show junkie?" He glared at Buster.

Unintimidated, Buster slowly reached into his hip pocket and withdrew his wallet. He flipped it open to show his gold detective's shield. "No, never watch 'em," he said. "Too inaccurate for my taste. I'm Buster Mayweather with the District of Columbia Metro Police Department." His voice was level, and his facial expression was neutral. Only the fact that he'd completely dropped the ghetto from his speech, and was sounding like the Rhode's Scholar he almost was told me that he was angry.

Holiday's posture stiffened further. "So, you're a cop. Well . . . Detective Mayweather, why should I bother having pictures taken of this?"

Jesus H. Christ, I thought, how in hell did this guy ever get to be chief of police.

Buster was saved from having to answer by the blond cop. "Uh, chief, we don't know how the victim died," he said. "So, we should treat this as a crime scene until the doc gets here and examines the body."

Holiday's cheeks turned red, and he glared at the young cop. I wouldn't want to be in that young man's shoes.

"Okay," he said, puffing up his chest. "Tape off the scene and go get the evidence kit from the car."

Buster's mouth opened. "You don't have a crime scene technician?"

"Lakeview's just a small town . . . detective. We don't have the budget you folks got down in DC. Hell, you're looking at a third of the town police force with the three of us." He glared at the EMTs. "Why don't you two go have a seat outside until the doc gets here."

The man glared back. "I think we should at least examine the body," he said. "You know, make sure the victim's not maybe still alive?"

The color in Holiday's cheeks got darker. He looked like he was about to have a stroke. He puffed his cheeks and then exhaled loudly. "Okay, just try not to disturb the scene, will you."

The young cop came back carrying a camera strapped around his neck, a bulky green case, and a roll of yellow crime scene tape. He put the case and tape on the floor just outside the freezer, waited until the male EMT had checked the body, shook his head and stepped away, and then began snapping photos of the body. I watched him work. His boss was an idiot, but the kid seemed to know what he was doing. He did long shots from the door and then from the opposite angle, close-up shots of various parts of the body, and shots in all directions from where the body lay. I noticed that he took several of the bruise on LeClerc's face. He came out of the freezer.

"Man, it's cold as a well digger's ass in Montana in there," he said, blowing on his fingers.

He knelt and opened the case. From inside it, he withdrew a small rectangular box that I recognized as a field fingerprint kit, a container of fine dark powder, a soft-bristle brush, and the sticky strips used to check for latent prints at crime scenes. He began by dusting the freezer door handle and the area immediately around it on both sides of the door. From a distance, I could see eight or ten smudges that could have been prints. He carefully lifted each smudge with one of the strips, which he labeled and put in a brown envelope that he'd also taken from the case. Even though I didn't think he would find anything useful, I had to give the kid credit for being thorough. He walked slowly along the aisle down the center of the freezer, stopped to dust the stack of boxes to the right of the corpse, shook his head when no prints appeared, moved on to the back of the freezer, turned and walked back, his attention focused on the area to the left of LeClerc's body.

Back outside the freezer, he jammed his hands under his arms and shook himself.

Holiday put his hands on his hips and blew out another gust of air. "Well, Cory, you gonna tell me what you found, or am I gonna have to play twenty questions?"

"Uh, sorry, chief, I just needed to warm up a bit. It's awful cold in there. Just sucks the heat right out of you." The kid blew on his fingers again. "Anyway, there's lots of prints on the door. I'll have to print everyone here to be able to compare . . . oh shit, I'll need to print the victim, too."

I felt sorry for the poor bastard. He had a choice between standing there and taking abuse from his pot-bellied boss or going back into the freezing cold with a corpse. Wisely, he chose the corpse.

As he turned to reenter the freezer, Holiday laid a meaty hand on his shoulder. "You see anything else, Cory?"

"No, chief. There's no sign of struggle. Nothing to indicate that anyone else but the victim was there, except for faint scuff marks on the floor, which were probably made by us. Nothing suspicious."

Holiday let his hand drop to his side. He had a smug look on his face. "Okay, go ahead and get your prints." He turned to Campbell. "The victim was your head chef, right?"

Campbell nodded. "Yes, *Vivienne LeClerc*

is, was, my head chef."

If Holiday noticed Campbell's dig at his depersonalization of the dead woman by referring to her as the 'victim,' he didn't show it.

"I reckon this'll put a bit of a damper on your opening tonight, won't it?"

"Why should it?"

"How you gonna open a restaurant without a head chef?"

Campbell's fists clenched. I didn't need a written guide to know how badly he wanted to smash those fists into Holiday's florid face. Not only was the man a lousy cop, but he was an insensitive son of a bitch to boot. Buster was standing next to me, and I could sense his tension as well. His friend was being abused. The old instincts kicked in. Campbell took a deep breath, and let it out slowly. He looked Holiday directly in the eye.

"As it happens, Walter Muncie's just as good as Vivienne . . . was, and he'll be able to hold things together until I can hire a new head chef."

"Dagnabit, that Campbell luck," Holiday said. "You fall into a pile of shit; you still come up smellin' like roses."

There was obviously some history between these two. Small town intrigue. People think small towns are idyllic, but they're not really. Whatever it was between them probably started before Campbell was even born.

Before he could respond to Holiday's

taunt, a short, rotund man with a fringe of white hair ringing his liver-spotted skull, and wearing a rumpled gray suit, came bustling into the kitchen.

"Where's the body?" He directed his question to Holiday, who pointed to the corpse on the floor of the freezer.

The new arrival turned to Campbell. His round, pink-cheeked face wore an expression of concern.

"How you holding up, Robert? That your chef, that lovely French gal?"

Campbell nodded.

"Doc, I need you to examine the body. See if you can tell me how she died, and when," Holiday said.

"Well now, unless she's got a bullet hole in her head or a knife sticking out of her back, I'm not likely to be able to tell you how she died until I get her on an autopsy table, *chief..*"

Another tense tableau. Damn, it looked like no one in this town got along with anyone else.

We stood there, silently waiting, as the doctor knelt and examined the corpse, starting at the head and working his way down, gently turning it to inspect the back. Finally, he stood, brushed at his rumpled trousers and came out of the freezer. Like the young cop, he blew on his fingers.

"Good Lord, an Eskimo would be right at home in there. It feels like twenty below."

Holiday shuffled from foot to foot, his brow furrowed. "Okay, doc, what can you tell me?"

"You know, Samuel, you always were too impatient." After blowing on his hands again, he turned toward Buster and me. "You two gentlemen must be friends of young Robert here." He extended a hand. "Forgive my cold hands. Welcome to Lakeview. It's not usually like this. I'm Jeremiah Johnson, one of three doctors in town, and the town coroner."

His hands were cold, but his grip was warm and his gaze was sincere.

"Look, Jeremiah, I don't have time to stand here while you play Welcome Wagon." Holiday sputtered as he spoke. "Unless you want the town council to take another look at their decision to make you the town's coroner, you'll give me your preliminary report."

Johnson seemed unfazed by Holiday's unprofessional outburst.

"Oh, Sam, Sam, that's just like you, using bluster and threats when a polite question would do. Okay, here's my preliminary report: a white female, no obvious signs of injury other than a square-shaped bruise on the left side of her head, no external signs of toxins, just signs of severe hypothermia. I won't know for sure until I get her on the table, but my guess is she froze to death."

Holiday smiled. It was the kind of smile that sends chills down your spine. "So, it's possible she went in the freezer to get something, slipped and hit her head, and froze to death before she came to?"

Johnson made a 'tut, tut' sound. "Don't go jumping to conclusions, Sam," he said. "Yeah, if she slipped and hit her head, knocking her unconscious, at the temperature in there she'd get frostbite, which her fingers and the tips of her ears show signs of, and dressed in light clothing like she is, her system wouldn't have been generating enough heat, she could've lasted six to eight hours, less depending on factors like her body mass, the presence of alcohol in the bloodstream, and things like that."

"So, you're saying it *could* be an accident?"

Johnson grunted. "Yeah, it could be an accident. I see no signs of struggle or other damage, but I won't know for certain until I do an autopsy."

"Okay, for now we'll just say possible accident and leave it at that," Holiday said. "Looks like you luck out again, Campbell. I don't have to close you down."

"Why would you have to close me down anyway?"

"Well, if it wasn't an accident, this would be a crime scene. Couldn't have people tramping all over it. Like I said, you've got that Campbell luck."

With that, he walked away. Johnson looked at his back, an expression of disgust on his face. "Let's hope it *is* an accident, because that clown couldn't find a bull in the middle of a china shop at noon." He blew at his hands again. "Okay, Robert, I'll have the EMTs transport her to my office. I'll put a rush on this. You got the name of her next of kin, to make arrangements for the remains?"

"Yeah, she has a sister who just emigrated from France. She lives in New York City. I'll have to call and inform her."

Johnson patted him on the shoulder. "Sorry about this, son. Terrible way to start your new business, an accident like this."

As he left to find the EMTs, I looked back at Vivienne's corpse, lying so serene-looking. If she'd been conscious when the hypothermia took hold, she'd have been curled into a fetal position. The way she was lying indicated that she was still unconscious when her heart stopped, probably unaware to what was happening. All the wine she'd had at dinner wouldn't have helped either. There's no such thing as a good way to die, but this, at least, would have been relatively painless.

So, why was I thinking it was no accident?

Charles Ray

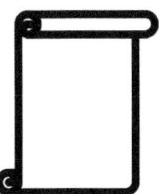

TEN

The EMTs had removed the body. The cops were gone. Walter Muncie arrived just as the ambulance was leaving, and nearly went into shock when Jerome Collins told him what had happened. He sagged back against the wall at the side of the dining room, his face as pale as rice paper.

"W-what happened?"

"We don't know," Campbell said. "You came back to work with her last night, right." Muncie nodded. "Was she okay?"

"She was f-fine when I left around ten. I mean, you know, she was tottering a little from all that wine, but hell, Vivienne could cook better drunk than anybody I know can do stone sober."

"You left her here alone?" Campbell's face was inches from Muncie's and his expression was a long way from kind.

Muncie recoiled as if struck. "Y-yeah. She told me to go home and g-get some sleep. She did that a lot, you know. I mean, what's to be scared of in this one-horse town?"

I understood his nervousness, in part. Learning that a colleague you'd just left has died is enough to unsettle anyone. But, something about the way he reacted bothered me. I just couldn't put my finger on what it was.

"That's okay, Walter," Campbell said. "Look, we still have to go ahead with preparations for tonight's opening; do you think you can handle the kitchen?"

Muncie stepped away from the wall, all traces of unease removed from his face. "Of course, Mr. Campbell, you can count on me. I learned a lot from . . . Vivienne. I'll make you proud."

"Good, then, get to it. Let me know if you need anything."

I had a lot of thoughts tumbling around in my head. A little itch was nagging at me. Something about all this was not right. If only I could pin down what that something was.

"Look, is there some place we can talk privately?" I said, taking in him and Buster. "Not that I don't trust the doctor's call, he seems like a straight shooter, but I wouldn't trust that police chief of yours to direct traffic."

Campbell looked at me, curiosity apparent in the way he narrowed his eyes to slits. "What? You think something's wrong?"

"I know that tone of voice," Buster said. "Al's got a hunch, and I trust his hunches."

"You don't think this was an accident?" His expression changed from curious to incredulous.

"I'd rather talk about that without too many other ears around, and, if it's okay with you, I'd like to include my partner, Heather, and Quincy in the discussion."

Campbell was shaking his head, now looking confused.

"Just listen to him," Buster said. "Al's hunches are as good as hard evidence, bro; even better in some cases."

"Uh, I guess we could use my office." Campbell still didn't look convinced. "It's at the other end of the building in back. We'd have privacy there."

I pulled out my cell phone and called Heather. When she answered, I told her to get Quincy and meet us at the restaurant. She's worked with me long enough to know when not to ask questions. She said they'd be there in ten minutes.

It was more like five minutes later that the five us were jammed into what Campbell called his office, a room no more than three times the size of a broom closet, with a desk, four chairs, a filing cabinet, and a three-shelf bookcase filled with black three-ring binders taking up most of the space.

Campbell gave Heather the chair behind his desk, and she immediately set up her laptop and booted it up—leave it to her not to *leave* it behind when going on what supposed to be a vacation. I imagine that if she was on a plane that had ditched at sea and was told she had to leave her laptop on board before she could get into the life raft, she'd stay on the plane rather than being separated from it. Campbell then insisted that Buster, Quincy, and I take the remaining seats, but since I was the one who'd called the meeting, and would be doing most of the talking, I opted to stand. I positioned myself at the edge of the desk, with Heather on my left, and the three men seated in a semi-circle in front of me.

"Okay, bro," Buster said. "Class is assembled, so school us."

For a moment, with the three men looking expectantly at me and Heather with her fingers poised over the keyboard of her laptop, I felt like an imposter. Who the hell did I think I was? Sure, I'd solved a few high profile cases, cases that had puzzled local and federal cops, but I'd also come pretty close to getting my ass shot off. Worse, a time or two, I'd almost gotten my friends hurt. Why did I always have to stand up when everyone else was sitting down? Of course, I knew the answer. I hate to see injustice. I have to speak for those who can't speak for themselves, because they're too weak, or like Vivienne LeClerc are dead. A few of things that bothered me about what I'd seen in the kitchen began to click into place. I might be wrong, but I was willing to bet my reputation that wasn't. I took a deep breath.

"Okay, what I'm about to say might come as a shock, so let me preface it with an apology if I offend any of this town's honored citizens," I said. "The doctor hasn't delivered his verdict yet, but I got the sense that he was leaning toward Vivienne's death being an accident."

Campbell raised his hand like a third grader wanting to go to the little boy's toilet. I nodded at him. "Well, it did look that way to me, too. After all, you saw how much she drank last night. It's entirely possible she went into the freezer, and in her inebriated state, slipped, fell and hit her head."

"That is possible, but in my opinion not probable," I said. "Allow me to explain why."

Charles Ray

ELEVEN

"Let's assume she went into the freezer alone," I said. "She's still a little woozy from the wine. She slips and hits her head, knocking herself out. What's the temperature in there?"

"It varies from minus 15 to minus 30 degrees," Campbell said.

"Okay, at that temperature, and with the alcohol she had in her blood, if she hit her head hard enough, she'd be unconscious long enough for her core temperature to drop to a fatal level. Even if she revived, which is doubtful, she'd probably be unable to move or call for help. In fact, let's assume she was alone in the building, so there'd be no help to call. By the time your guy Guptar arrived, she'd be dead."

Campbell got an 'ah ha, gotcha' look on his face. "That's what I said. She was too drunk. She fell and hit her head. An accident, right?"

I let him gloat a full ten seconds.

"Wrong." His face fell. "Let's start with the obvious. If she hit her head, how'd the freezer door close? Does it close automatically?"

"No, when it's open, it stays that way for safety and convenience. It's constructed that way to keep someone from accidentally getting locked in, although it can be opened from the inside, but the main reason is that it'd be a bitch, er, excuse me Heather." She just smiled at him. "It'd be a hassle to have to keep opening and closing it if you had to take several frozen items out and you couldn't make it in one trip."

His expression started changing. Comprehension was slowly dawning.

"So, if she went in, she wouldn't have closed the door, and if she fell and knocked herself out, she *couldn't* have closed it."

"Shit," he said.

"That's just the matter of the door," I said. "The position of the body, and that bruise on the side of her head's another problem."

Now, it was Buster's turn to look puzzled. "What did you see that the rest of us didn't bro?"

"She was lying face down with her head toward the back of the freezer, and the bruise was on the left side of her head; face actually, looked like something square and possibly flat hit her in the temple area."

"Yeah, we all saw that."

"But, the only things in that freezer that are square and flat were on her *left* side. The bags of ice on her left would've made an irregular bruise, not an almost perfectly square or rectangular one."

Now, it was Buster's turn to say, "Shit!"

"Finally, My *pièce de résistance*," I said, bowing at the waist. "She was   wearing those flat sole, canvas bottom shoes that she had on in the dining room. I can't see her slipping and falling with those things on. The freezer floor wasn't that slick."

Quincy smiled. Buster returned my bow, and after straightening, turned to Campbell. "Didn't I tell you this dude was a pistol? I been a cop for over ten years, and I didn't notice *any* of that."

Campbell was smiling too, and shaking his head. "Chief Holiday's gonna have puppies when we drop this bit of news on him."

Quincy and Heather looked confused when Campbell and Buster started laughing.

I did my imitation of a traffic cop, and they finally stopped—sort of, they put their hands over their mouths and made 'snuffling' sounds. "Okay, guys, grow up," I said. To Heather and Quincy I said, "It's an inside joke. I'll explain it to you later. For now folks, I don't think we should tell the chief of police."

"Why not?" Campbell asked.

"You heard him. He was ready to jump all over this being an accident. He's like anyone else who already has his mind made up, unless you hit him in the face with some real hard evidence, he's not going to listen. I don't know what you think of him, Bob, but in my opinion, the man's just plain stupid. If he was a turkey, he'd drown standing in the rain."

Campbell snickered. "I can't argue with you about him being stupid. The only reason he's the chief is because his late daddy was chief before him. I think the old man had a file on every member of the city council. He arm twisted them to let him hire Samuel, and when he retired, old Sam was promoted to chief. They didn't even look for a qualified candidate. Hell, every cop on the force is more qualified than he is. Okay, I see your point. We can't tell him now. So, what do we do?"

All doubt had vanished. Everyone was on board. Well, Campbell was on board; the others I knew would go along, but this was his town, his problem, and if he didn't want me butting in it would've been a problem. I turned to Heather.

"Heather, I want you to do a full background check on Vivienne LeClerc for starters. Bob, can you let Heather see your personnel files?" He nodded. "Great. Along with LeClerc, do checks on Walter Muncie and Gavin Laine."

"I guess I can understand you checking Gavin's background," Campbell said. "He's my competitor, and hasn't made any bones about not wanting me to open. Killing my head chef might achieve his aims, but I don't really see him as a killer. I'm confused, though. Why do you want to check on Walter?"

"First rule of investigation, Bob, check the people closest to the victim; anyone who benefits from the victim's demise, and unfortunately, Muncie fits the bill."

"Wha—"

"He's right, bro," Buster said. "Most homicides are committed by family members, boyfriends or girlfriends, business partners, in other words, people closest to the vic. And, look what happened; you put Muncie in charge of the kitchen."

"But, I've known Walter for years, and he and Vivienne have worked closely together for the past nine months. They got along so well. I can't see him killing her."

"Hey, being close don't mean jack sometimes. Remember that Special Forces doctor, Jeffery MacDonald, killed his wife and two daughters back in 1970? What I remember reading is it started out as an argument with his wife, and ended up with him clubbing and stabbing all three of them to death and trying to claim some drugged up cult guys broke into his house and did it. No, bro, Al's right. Look first at the people close, if for no other reason than to exclude them."

"And, for that reason," I said. "We need to do checks on all your employees."

Campbell stood and walked across to the filing cabinet. He opened the second drawer and withdrew eight manila folders.

"Here are the files on everyone," he said, handing them to me. I passed them to Heather who opened the first one and began pecking at her keyboard. "My own file is included in that bunch. Not that I'd have any reason to hurt Vivienne, but if you're going to check, you should check everyone, right?"

I smiled and nodded. My opinion of him went up another couple of notches. Of course I would've had Heather check him out, but having him offer himself up like that showed that he understood what we were doing, and pretty much removed him from any list of suspects I might develop.

"Thanks for being cooperative. We'll try not to be too intrusive. For the time being, it might be best not to let your staff know we're checking on them."

"You don't seriously suspect any of them, even Walt, could've hurt Vivienne, do you?"

Going into a case, it's always best to keep an open mind. Everyone's a suspect, but it's a mistake to focus to much on any one person at the outset, because doing so could blind you to information leading to the true perpetrator. The cops, unfortunately, do this quite often. A crime occurs, they encounter someone whose profile fits who they *think* would commit such a crime, and everything else gets ignored. More than one innocent person has been jailed because of this. For that reason, even though a gremlin in the back of my mind kept whispering Walter Muncie's name, I stifled the urge to think of him as the main suspect.

"At this point," I said. "I, we, don't know enough to speculate. We just have to dig until we hit something interesting, and then follow where that leads." I turned to Heather. "Which reminds me, don't forget to do a background on our police chief."

Campbell's mouth dropped open. "Surely you don't suspect the chief of police of killing my chef?"

I held my hands up, close to my chest, palms out. "Open mind, remember? But, no, I don't think the chief of police sneaked in here last night and killed Vivienne. But, he's a factor we have to consider as we look into this, and a cardinal rule is to know your opposition. At some point, we'll have to involve him, and to do that effectively, we need to know as much as possible about him."

"What do you need from me?" Quincy asked.

He'd been sitting quietly the whole time, but I knew he'd taken it all in. "Quincy, you're our legal advisor," I said. "My PI license is DC, Maryland, and Virginia, and Buster's a DC cop out of his jurisdiction. So, I need you to monitor and make sure we stay on the right side of the law."

"Got it," he said.

Buster grunted. His way of saying he was in.

Heather was ignoring us all, busy coaxing information out of the ether.

Campbell sat there looking from one of us to the other with a perplexed look on his face, but he'd already joined the team the minute he handed me those files.

My dream team was formed, and the game was afoot.

TWELVE

While Heather continued to do her online investigating, Buster and I decided to have a chat with each of the employees. We debated splitting them up and going at them one-on-one, and then decided to tag team them. With two people doing the questioning, especially two people who've worked together as long as Buster and I have, the approach can be alternated, with one being pushy and hard, while the other comes across as warm and friendly. It might be cliché, but the good cop, bad cop routine actually works. If a person's thrown off balance by a harsh question, and someone steps in to defend them, the instinct is to cling to the person offering help.

By mutual consent, we decided to start with Muncie; not because he was a prime suspect, but because, as far as we knew, he was the last person to see LeClerc alive.

We found him in the kitchen, sitting on a stool at the long mixing table in the center of the room reading a cookbook.

"Boning up on recipes?" I asked as we came up behind him.

He jerked around so violently, he sent the book sliding halfway across the table.

"Shit, you scared me. Do you always sneak up on people like that?"

His face was red and he was breathing hard.

"Sorry. I guess you were so engrossed in what you were reading you didn't hear us come in."

"Yeah, okay. I guess I'm a little jumpy. I mean, after what happened to Vivienne, it's to be expected, right?"

Not if it was really an accident, I thought, but I said, "Yeah, guess you're right. Say, mind if we ask a few questions. Your boss asked my friend and me to put together information for the insurance claim."

Okay, I made that lie up on the fly. It just came to me, but it sounded credible. I glanced at Buster, who was smiling and nodding his head.

"Yeah," Muncie said. "Whaddya wanna know?"

The key to a successful interrogation, or

any kind of interview for that matter, is to put the subject at ease. Too many cops, having watched too many 'Dirty Harry' movies, come at it with a make-my-day attitude, resulting in the subject either clamming up and asking for a lawyer, or feeding them a load of crap they think the questioner wants to hear just to make the annoyance or pain go away—yeah, some even resort to physical methods to extract information, which any interrogator with an ounce of sense or experience can tell you is the wrong way to go about getting useful information. With Buster at my side I had no need to put on a bad-guy act. All he had to do was scowl and most perps started pissing their pants just thinking about what he *might* do. For our initial run at Muncie, though, we decided to go good cop, good cop.

"How long have you worked for Robert Campbell?" I asked.

"Six months now, ever since he decided to open this place. He hired me before he hired that . . . Vivienne."

I let that almost Freudian slip go, saving it for later.

"Did he hire you as head chef?"

He blinked. "Uh, no, not exactly. I mean, I can cook. I graduated from the Cochran Culinary School in Buffalo. Paid my own way through. He hired Vivienne the week after he hired me. Said he wanted a chef with international experience at the start. Lot of the people up here, the ones that live here and the tourists, are pretty snobby. They pay good money for that kinda shit."

"When he hired you, did you think you might eventually be head chef?"

"Well, he didn't really say at first, just that he wanted to hire me as a cook. That it'd be good having a local on the staff as a chef, you know. I was born right here in Lakeview. I guess I thought maybe that meant I'd be the top dog in the kitchen. Shoulda known better though. The upper crust 'round here only take mixing with us lesser folk so far."

I was sensing a lot of pent up anger, but it was hard to tell who it was aimed at.

"Did you and Vivienne get along?"

His gaze flickered momentarily, up and to the left, and then settled back on a point just past my chin. "Uh, yeah, we got along okay."

His eye movements and failure to look me in the eye were pretty clear indicators that he was lying through his teeth. But, it wasn't enough. I'd only met Vivienne LeClerc briefly, and she'd made something of a negative impression on me. For one, she drank too much. I'm not into the temperance movement; hell, I drink; but, she was pouring wine down her throat at dinner like it was water, and just before going back to work. But, the thing about her that I imagine really grated on people was her casually dismissive attitude toward Americans, an attitude I've noticed in a lot of Europeans, especially

French. I'd ignored it, because she hadn't said anything directly to me, but it was there, and like dust motes that you can barely see, but that tickle your nose and make you sneeze, irritating.

"So, when you left her here last night, what time was it?"

"I told you already, it was around ten."

"And, she was the only other person in the place at the time?"

"Yeah, I mean, the wait staff didn't need to be around that late until we officially open. They've been knocking off at six."

"Do you know anyone who might want to hurt her?"

The eye movement thing again, only this time his gaze settled on a spot to the opposite side of my face. "Nah, she got along with everybody."

"Okay, thanks. Look, if you think of anything, come find us."

"Sure, I'll do that."

He quickly turned back to his cookbook. I didn't expect him to be looking for us anytime soon.

Our next stop was Sanjay Guptar. We found him in the bar, a rectangular space partially curtained off from the main dining room. It had twelve barstools, and six of those chest-high, circular tables you see at some cocktail parties for guests who can't hold their cocktails and plates of food and talk at the same time. He was sitting on the barstool farthest from the entrance, polishing silver. Equal sized stacks of polished and unpolished silver were on the bar in front of him. He looked up as we entered. A broad smile lit up his dark face.

"Gentlemen, welcome to my office," he said. "May I get you anything to drink? We have not fully stocked the bar, but there is tea and coffee, and of course, water."

"No, we're good," I said. "But, we would like a few minutes of your time."

"Of course, how may I help you?"

"You found LeClerc, Vivienne's body, right?"

He winced and looked down at the fork he was still polishing.

"Yes, I did. What a horrible experience that was I am telling you. When I opened the freezer and saw her lying there, I did not know at first what I was seeing. Then, when I realized what . . . who it was, I think I must have yelled . . . well, actually, as Jerome said, I screamed like a little girl." His eyes kept shifting from me to his hands. He rubbed nervously at the fork, polishing the same area over and over.

"I know that must have been a terrible experience for you, so we'll only take a few minutes of your time. Mr. Campbell has asked us to put together a report for the insurance company, you know, liability issues."

He stopped polishing the fork and looked

directly at me.

"Of course, what do you wish to know?"

"How well did you know Vivienne LeClerc?"

He held the fork up, turning it from side to side. The overhead light, reflecting off the handle caused a flicker to slide back and forth across his dark, blemish-free cheeks. Then, he sighed and put it down with the other polished forks, knives and spoons.

"Ms. LeClerc was not an easy person to get to know. I am but a lowly waiter, hardly someone she would spend time with."

"Did she spend time with anyone?"

He leaned forward and folded one hand over the other with his elbows propped on the bar. He rested his chin on the back of his hand.

"It is hard to say that she spent time *with* anyone," he said. "She spent most of her time in the kitchen, just her and Mr. Muncie."

"So, most of her time was spent with him?"

His smile was rueful; there was no happiness in it. "Like I said, sir, she did not spend time *with* people. She was a very demanding chef. Unfortunately, Mr. Muncie did not always meet her expectations."

I was listening to his words, but more than that, I was watching him as he spoke. Buster was listening and would help me recall what I needed to know of what he said. I was more interested in watching his facial expressions and body language, in particular, the micro-expressions, those fleeting eye movements, lip quirks, shoulder twitches, that people aren't even aware of making, that are more reliable than a polygraph in indicating deception. Guptar's clipped accent marked him as a foreigner who came to the U.S. in his late teens or early adulthood, but I couldn't be absolutely sure, because South Asians, especially Indians, tended to keep their kids under tight control and in as much of a native environment as possible. As a consequence, except for those who were born in the U.S., or arrived as infants, they tended to have pronounced accents. Not as bad as I'd encountered the one time I went to India back in the mid-1990s, when I'd been unable to understand their English, but still pronounced. Fortunately, micro-expressions aren't culturally based; only total psychopaths, people who have no right-wrong switch in their brains, have micro-expressions that are hard, or impossible, to read accurately.

Guptar was clearly upset, but he exhibited no signs of lying.

"Are you saying that LeClerc didn't get along with anyone?"

"It is not that she did not get along with anyone. Except for criticizing what she saw as our deficiencies as uncivilized barbarians, and those are her exact words on more than one occasion, the only person she bothered to engage in conversation with was Mr. Campbell, and I did not see her do that very often."

I talked him for a few more minutes, confirming his account of when he and the others had left the place the night before and when that morning's arrival time. I thanked him for his time; Buster just grunted at him; and went in search of our next subject.

Jerome Collins was near the entrance to the restaurant, arranging tablecloths, centerpieces, and napkins on tables. When he saw Buster and me approaching, he stopped what he was doing and waited, his arms loose at his side.

"I guess you guys wanna talk to me now, huh?"

"How'd you know?" Buster asked.

"I passed Walter in the back when I was coming from the linen storage. He said you guys were doing some kinda insurance report for the boss."

Small towns, small places, there's really nothing secret. It didn't hurt, though. Now, we didn't have to keep repeating our cover story.

"Okay, then," I said. "We'll try not to take too much of your time. We just have a few questions."

He leaned his narrow hips against the table and folded his arms across his chest.

"Shoot. What do you want to know?"

"Let's start with how well you knew

Vivienne LeClerc."

"Miss Lady? I knew her name and what she looked like, but I don't think she ever even said hello to me since the boss hired her."

"I understand most of the rest of you were hired before she was?"

"You got that right. And, before she got here, we all got along pretty well. Old Walt, he tries to act all boojie, but he's just trailer trash that managed to get a degree from some cooking school, and before Miss Vivienne came, he'd even come out here and take breaks with us. 'Course, she put a stop to that. Said, the sous chef shouldn't be fraternizing. Can you believe that shit?"

In such a small establishment, that kind of stratification was hard to imagine, but this was the second time I'd heard it. Vivienne LeClerc was not a well-liked person. That, of course, made almost anyone she came into contact with a viable suspect.

"So, what was their relationship like, Vivienne and Walter, I mean?"

"Now, that's the funny thing," he said. "She didn't want him hanging with us, but she considered him too low in the food chain to be anything but her whipping boy. Man, a few times when I was getting stuff from the supply closet, I heard her reaming his poor ass something terrible."

I filed that away to follow up on. Muncie hadn't mentioned it, which put a minus sign next to his name on my list of possible suspects.

"Did she get along with anyone?" I asked.

"She seemed okay with Mr. Campbell, in a suck-up sorta way. But, I never thought she meant it, you know, just being nice to the dude that signs the paycheck, know what I mean? I mean, that chick didn't really seem to *like* anybody. When she first came, I thought she avoided me 'cause I'm black, but then I saw she was the same with everybody."

"Well, thanks for talking to us Jerome. You've been a big help. Where's your colleague, Sunyi?"

"She's doing inventory in the supply room. We rotate that duty 'cause it's always so dusty back there. Anything else you want to know?"

I told him no, and he went back to arranging tables. I didn't completely eliminate him as a suspect, but my gut told me that he had no real reason to harm LeClerc.

We found Sunyi Kim just where Collins had said she'd be, in the middle of the storage room, walking from shelf to shelf, with a clipboard in her hand. When Buster and I entered, she turned, blew a lock of raven hair from in front of her eyes and smiled.

"You wanna ask me about Vivienne, right?"

Well, of course she knew. After all, Muncie, the first person we'd talked to and the well of gossip it seems, worked in the kitchen not all that far away, and she would've had to pass the kitchen to get to the supply room.

"Yeah," I said. "How well did you know her?"

"I don't know her. She never speak to me, never even say good morning."

Now, that surprised me. I would have figured that the only two women in the place would've at least been on casual speaking terms.

"I'm starting to get the feeling that Ms. LeClerc didn't get along with anyone."

She put a hand on her hip and cocked her head to one side. "She not have fights with anyone, except she always screaming at Walter. She remind me of my mother. She always screaming at people, too, and for same reason. They don't do things the way she do them, so they wrong. Vivienne always saying Walter not belong in kitchen in fine restaurant; he should be fry cook in diner. The rest of us, though, she just ignore like we pieces of furniture."

"So, other than Walter, can you think of anyone who would want to hurt her?"

"What do you mean, other than Walter? I don't think he hurt her. I don't think Walter would hurt a fly. I don't think anybody like her, but I don't know anybody who would want to . . . why somebody put her in freezer like that?"

I didn't have an answer to her question. I didn't have the answers to a lot of questions. I just thanked her for her time and we left.

The restaurant's accountant, Jefferson Aldercott, worked from home, but Campbell had called him to come in. Buster and I interviewed him in Campbell's office. Because he was seldom in the restaurant, he had little to offer. He rarely, he said, went into the kitchen, and had only met LeClerc once and hadn't formed an opinion of her one way or another.

So, we'd spent the good part of the morning, and, other than learning that Walter Muncie and the deceased had a troubled relationship, not a lot to show for our efforts.

I told Campbell that we were going back to the hotel to study what we'd learned. Heather was happy with that, preferring to work in the privacy and comfort of her room, and Quincy said he'd be at the pool working on his tan if we needed him.

Charles Ray

THIRTEEN

Buster and I decided to huddle in a quiet corner of the spa's huge lobby rather than either of our rooms; in mine, Sandra was taking a nap, and in his, Alma had the twins quietly coloring and didn't want the mood broken. Heather, with her laptop tucked under her arm like a purse, went off to her room where she'd have no distractions, and Quincy went to change into his swim trunks.

We found a little conversation nook, a low round marble table and four wrought iron chairs, tucked in behind two gigantic vases containing ferns whose leaves completely blocked the view of the table from elsewhere in the lobby. As we sat, Buster took a notepad from his shirt pocket and put it on the table.

"I don't know about you," he said. "But, this Walter Muncie character's looking good for this in my book."

"I agree that he certainly has motive, if his colleagues' accounts of the abuse he suffered from LeClerc are true. But, I don't want to rush to judgment. From their stories, they all had a reason not to like her."

He nodded and ran a hand over the stubble on his square jaw. "Yeah, you're right there. She didn't strike me as the warm and fuzzy type, but from what they said, she was a real bitch."

True enough, but I knew he thought the same as I did; she still didn't deserve to be knocked out and left in a freezer to die.

"So, what we have to do is take each individual and pick their lives apart. We need to find out what their relationship was with the victim and their movements last night to see if they could've been in the restaurant around the time she went into the freezer."

"Well, we know Muncie was with her at least part of the time," he said. "He left here with her."

"Right, but we only have their word that the other three had already left before LeClerc and Muncie went back. For that matter, we need to check that accountant out."

He sat back in his chair. "You're kidding,

right? That dude's just a number cruncher."

"Hey, remember back when I was just starting out as a private investigator? What'd you tell me? Never ignore anyone connected with a victim, no matter how remote."

"Oh yeah, I did say that, didn't I? Okay, Aldercott stays on the suspect list."

There was one other name that needed to be on that list, but I wasn't sure how Buster would react to it.

"We also need to put your friend, Robert, on that list, you know that, right?"

He rubbed his stubble again and winced as he looked at me.

"Yeah, I know in my gut he didn't do it, but a rule's a rule. He was close to the victim, so he has to be on the list. Okay, what do we do next?"

"Well, first, I give Heather the list of suspects." I took out my phone and dialed her mobile. When she answered, I told her to add Aldercott and Campbell to the list of people she was researching, listened a second or two, and then broke the connection.

"What'd she say?"

"She'd already added their names," I said.

"Girl learns well." He laughed. "So what do we do, wait for her to come up with something?"

"Not much else we can do, I suppose." Then, I had an idea. "You know, I'm curious about Vivienne LeClerc. I wonder if we could get a peek at her living quarters."

Buster's brow wrinkled. "I don't know, bro. Neither one of us have any authority to be poking around up here."

Of course, I knew that, but my curiosity was aroused. Here was a woman, dead under what were, to me, suspicious circumstances, not really liked by anyone. Sure, Walter Muncie was a prime suspect as the target of much of her venomous ire according to his coworkers, but I had a feeling something was missing. Until Heather came up with something we could use, the only other avenue that came to mind was getting to know the victim. Sometimes, understanding the victim was the key to understanding the crime. And, the local cops weren't treating it like a crime—yet.

"Let's talk to your friend anyway. Maybe he knows where she lived, and can get us in. Hey, it's not like we're disturbing a crime scene or anything, since the locals haven't called it a crime yet."

His brow wrinkles disappeared. "Good point. I suppose if Bob vouches for us, her landlord might let us poke around."

We were just about to stand when a shadow fell across the table. We looked to see Samuel Holiday, his thumbs hooked in his gun belt and a scowl on his face, looking down at us.

"Campbell said I'd find you two here," he said.

"Okay, chief, you found us," Buster said. "What can we do for you?"

He raised his right hand and stabbed his forefinger at Buster. "You can quite nosing around in something that's none of your business, is what you can do."

"Why, chief, whatever are you talking about?"

"Don't play games with me, *detective*. I don't know how you folks down in Washington do things, but up here, we respect jurisdiction, and I don't have to remind you that you have *no* jurisdiction here in my town." He turned the finger toward me. "And, as for you, you're not licensed as a PI in the state of New York. Now, if you know what's good for you, the both of you will keep your noses out of this case. Am I clear, or do I have to put in a call to your chief?"

Buster returned the man's scowl with a stony gaze. "You're as clear as can be, chief. I assure you I am not involving myself in any of your police work."

"Is that so? Then, why the hell are you two going around questioning people about that French woman's death?"

"Detective Mayweather's a friend of Mr. Campbell," I said. "And Mr. Campbell asked us to put together a report for his insurance company. Something to do with his liability policy, I believe."

"Yeah, Campbell said the same thing just now when I stopped in at his place, but I ain't buying it, not one bit. So, gentlemen, consider yourselves warned."

He spun, his belly jiggling, and walked away.

"Now, that was strange," Buster said.

Strange indeed. How had Holiday learned so quickly that we were nosing around? One of the people we spoke to must have told him, but the question in my mind was, why?, why would our routine questions on behalf of the dead woman's employer be interesting, or disturbing, enough that someone would tell the chief of police, and why the chief of police. As Alice said when she started to grow after eating a magic food in *Alice in Wonderland*, curiouser and curiouser.

FOURTEEN

We were on our way across the lobby when Heather came rushing from the elevator clutching a notepad. She intercepted us at the exit. Her face was flushed with excitement.

"What's up partner?" I asked.

She reached us just as a town police car drove past the entrance, Chief Samuel Holiday seated, like some ancient potentate, in the back seat. She stared wide-eyed through the big glass doors.

"What's up, Heather?" Buster asked. "You look like you just saw a ghost."

She blinked and turned to face us, her expression now all business.

"No, not a ghost, but I did just see an interesting subject, and I have some interesting little tidbits I thought you'd like to know."

That got my attention. I turned back toward our little conversation nook.

"Shall we adjourn to our office and discuss it?"

She bowed slightly. "Lead the way, kind sir."

Once we were seated around the table behind the tall ferns, Heather wasted no time.

"I haven't found anything useful on the live workers at Fantastic Fusion," she said. "But, I did find some interesting stuff on Vivienne LeClerc, the victim, and one other person of interest."

I thought about the way she'd looked through those doors. "Our chief of police?" I asked.

"The one and only."

"Tell us," Buster said.

"First, our victim, Vivienne LeClerc. It took some digging, but what I found on her puts a whole new light on this case." She stopped talking and looked from one of us to the other with a Cheshire cat-smile on her face. Beside me, Buster made a quiet growling noise deep in his throat. Heather was enjoying this. Finally, when even I was about to say 'get on with it,' she leaned forward and resumed speaking. "I had a devil of a time finding anything on her," she said. "I mean, it was like she didn't exist, except for the news articles announcing her hiring to be head chef of the new Fantastic Fusions Restaurant."

"What's so surprising about that? She's from France," Buster said.

Heather looked at him as if he'd dangled a participle or split an infinitive, whatever the hell that is. "That makes no difference," she said in a hectored school teacher-voice. "The Internet doesn't care about borders, and except for a few countries like China and Russia that try to control what's on it inside their borders, it can be accessed by anyone from anywhere as long as they have a computer and a satellite link. That also means that no matter where you're from, unless it's a remote Amazon village, your life's likely to be captured in an electronic file."

After a decade of working with Heather I'd come to understand and appreciate that inescapable fact. Our lives in the technological age, from birth to death and beyond, are captured in electronic files as we go about our daily activities, buying groceries, enrolling in school, getting a driver's license, applying for a mortgage, it doesn't matter how innocuous, the things we do are recorded and stored, on paper and electronically, just sitting there waiting for someone to come along and sniff them out.

And, there's no one better at sniffing things out than Heather Bunche. I'd hired her straight out of secretarial school shortly after I started the firm because paperwork has never been my strong point. In addition to being a crackerjack administrator, though, it turned out that she'd been something of a computer nerd in high school, and had taught herself how to work the electronic devices like John Coultrane played a saxophone. That skill, added to her little book containing the contact information of former classmates, most of whom were now working the front offices of many of DC's movers and shakers, people willing to share little tidbits of information with her, she was an information magnet.

"Are you suggesting that our victim wasn't really named Vivienne LeClerc?" I said.

"Unless she was living in a cave, there would have to be a record of her somewhere. I mean, she came here from France according to Buster's friend, so there'd be an immigration record, but I come up with nada. I even called a friend in ICE, and she said she couldn't find a record of Vivienne LeClerc ever entering the country."

If Immigration and Customs Enforcement, known as ICE, had no record of Vivienne LeClerc entering the U.S., it was a pretty safe bet she never had, at least not legally. After the 9/11 terrorist attacks and the establishment of the Department of

Homeland Security, immigration procedures had tightened. They weren't absolutely foolproof, but the chances of a French national entering the United States to work as a chef not being recorded in the system were pretty slim.

"Okay, so we have to assume that Vivienne LeClerc was either an illegal alien, or a con woman." I looked at Buster. "That makes it all the more important that we get into her place and look around."

"While you're at it," Heather said. "See if you can find out if she owns a computer, and if she does, get me access to it."

"Yeah, I get it. See if you can ID her through her email," Buster said. He might not be as up on computers as Heather, but he had a sharp investigative mind.

"That and her Internet searches," Heather said. "Now, get out there and get me that computer."

"Whoa," I said. "You said you had something on one other person of interest."

"Oh yeah, almost forgot. I ran across some pretty interesting stuff on the chief of police."

Buster had started to rise. He sat back down.

"Spill, girl," he said.

"I looked into Holiday's background like you asked. His father was a career cop, rose from patrolman to chief of police in just under twenty years, and held that job for decades. Holiday was an only child, his mother died when he was in high school. When he graduated, daddy hired him as a patrolman." She opened the notepad and quickly perused her precise script. "From what I could dig up he was just a so-so cop, but still managed to get regular promotions, making it to sergeant in fifteen years. When the old man retired, it came as a surprise to everyone when Holiday was appointed chief to replace him. He's been about as so-so as chief as he was when he was a patrolman, but has still managed to hang onto the job."

Buster grunted. "No real surprises there, kid. It's a small town, and in small towns people tend to support each other. I imagine the townspeople keep old Holiday because of his father."

"Probably," she said. "The old man, according to a few news sites I found, was a good, solid cop, liked by everyone, and squeaky clean."

"So, what's the surprising thing you found out?" I asked.

"The Holidays were solid middle-income, working class folks. Until recently, Holiday lived in the house he was born in. He got married to his high school sweetheart right after they made him chief five years ago, and they moved in with his father. The surprising part is this; about four years ago, Holiday and his wife got divorced, and then just over two years ago, he remarried. He then moved out of his father's house, bought a new house, and it's a serious upgrade, a mansion in the ritziest section of town. In addition, he traded in his old Ford Fairlane for a Mercedes 500XL."

"That must have cost some serious cash," Buster said. "He's gotta be mortgaged up to his eyeballs."

"That, my friend is the most interesting part," she said. "I dived deep into his financials and can't find evidence of a mortgage or car payment, *and* his credit card charges are more each month than I make in half a year, but he has no outstanding credit card balances. Oh yeah, and he has nearly a quarter million in a money market account that, coincidentally was opened six months ago."

Buster whistled. I sucked in air. Partly at the import of what Heather was saying, and in a small part thinking of what she'd had to do to get that information. Of course, there are some things I don't bother asking her, because I don't really want to know. I'm just glad she's one of the good guys.

Buster was shaking his head and scowling. I knew what he was thinking, because I was thinking the same thing.

Dirty cop.

Charles Ray

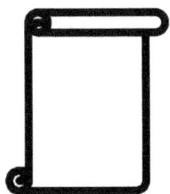

FIFTEEN

After dropping her bombshell, Heather snapped her notebook shut and excused herself to go back to her room to see what else she could ferret out. Buster and I sat in silence for several seconds, watching the elevator doors close on her.

Finally, Buster broke the silence.

"Shit, I hate dirty cops." He slammed his meaty fist into the table, causing it to vibrate. "You put on that badge, the public trusts that you'll be there to protect 'em. Anybody who betrays that trust is lower than whale shit."

"Can't say I disagree with you, amigo, but just like the rest of the population, a certain percentage of people with badges are likely to be bad."

He gave me a pained look.

"I know it, but it don't make it any easier to take."

"Well, other than him getting in the way of us finding out who killed Vivienne LeClerc, it's not really our problem."

"Yeah, I know. Okay, what now?"

I stood. "Let's go talk to your friend and see if we can get into LeClerc's lodgings."

He was silent as we left the hotel, crossed the parking lot and entered the quiet restaurant. He said nothing as I explained to Campbell that we wanted to take a look at where LeClerc lived. That turned out to be easier than I'd feared. It turned out that the Campbells were heavily invested in local real estate, and Campbell had rented one of his properties to LeClerc until she decided if she wanted to buy a place. He gave us the address and a key.

The small Cape Cod, a white affair with bright blue trim and a green slate roof, was on a side street at the north end of town, almost within walking distance of the spa if you were in to power walking. We drove in my bug. The house had a small detached garage and a neatly-kept lawn. I pulled the Volkswagen up near the garage door, killed the engine and we got out.

It was a quiet neighborhood. Mostly smaller ranch-style houses and Cape Cods, with not much vehicular or foot traffic except for an old man walking his mixed breed dog and a Post Office van delivering mail. It drove past LeClerc's mailbox without stopping.

Just out of curiosity I peeked through the small window of the garage door. Except for a few lawn tools hanging on hooks, and a lawnmower at the far end, it was empty. I made a mental note to have Heather check and see if LeClerc had a car, and if so, where it might be.

We walked to the front door. I paused before inserting the key. The only sounds now that the Post Office van was out of sight were birds chirping noisily. Except for the fact that the houses on both sides of the street were only twenty feet or so apart, it reminded me of home. I half expected to see a deer come prancing around the side of the house. I inserted the key and turned. The lock hardly made a sound, and the door opened smoothly.

We entered a small living room. Neat, but inexpensive furniture was neatly arranged, and except for a little dust on the coffee table top, the room was neat as a pin. Too neat. It didn't look lived in at all. There were no pieces of junk mail on the coffee table; no crumpled paper in the little round metal trash can next to the sofa; nothing to indicate that anyone had recently been here. In the kitchen, it was the same. No dishes in the sink. The cabinets above the sink had a few boxes of dry cereal, all but two unopened, a box of instant rice, and a box of crackers. The pantry had a few cans of sardines, baked beans, and spaghetti. I looked in the refrigerator. It contained a half empty one-gallon plastic container of skim milk, a container of orange juice and an egg carton with two eggs missing.

"What does this place say to you?" I asked Buster.

"She was a neat freak?"

"No, not that. What don't you see that you should be seeing?"

He looked around, his brow furrowed. "Don't look like she spent much time here."

"That's true, but don't you think a professional chef, even one that wasn't at home much, would have more . . . food preparation stuff in her kitchen?"

"Uh, yeah, I hadn't thought about that."

"Right. Now, let's take a look at the rest of the house."

The place had two small bedrooms. The first had a small single bed covered by a blue spread and looked as if it'd never been used. In the second, though, we found where Vivienne LeClerc *lived,* and it was shocking.

Her bedroom was completely different than the rest of the house. Calling it messy would have been a gross understatement. It was a mess. Articles of clothing, including underwear that most women didn't like having on public view, were scattered everywhere. The dresser across from the foot of the bed had makeup containers, hairbrush, and comb in a jumble on top. The bed looked like it hadn't been made, or had a change of linen, in a long time. And, to top it all off, the place smelled like a locker room. Hardly what I would have expected the bedroom of a woman, and a chef at that, to look and smell like, it was more like that of a teenaged boy.

In the far left corner, next to the closet door, were a tiny desk and a folding chair. A laptop computer that was plugged into the wall and connected to the phone jack was on the desk. I unplugged the computer and wrapped the two cords around it. Buster gave me a funny look.

"Heather said she wanted to look through it," I said. "Check the closet."

He opened the closet. Women's clothing hung askew on the rod, and several pairs of shoes were in a ragged row at the back of the closet. In front of the shoes were two 12-inch high stacks of spiral-bound books. I looked down. The covers of the books at the top of the stacks identified them as cookbooks, the kind you can find in the book and magazine section of a big drugstore.

"Well, at least she got cookbooks," he said.

I picked one up. *Desserts for all Occasions* it said on the cover. I flipped it open. The recipes were your standard cake, pie, and cookie recipes with nicely done photos and serving instructions.

"These are cookbooks for ordinary people,

not a so-called master chef," I said.

"You sure about that?"

"Pretty sure, but let's take 'em and have Heather take a look, or maybe Alma or Sandra. I'll bet they could tell us if these are the kind of cookbooks a restaurant chef would own."

"Okay, but I'm not lugging all of them. You gotta take a few."

I put the laptop under my left arm. "Okay, give me three or four of 'em."

We were heading back to the living room when the young black cop from the morning stepped into the hallway with his gun drawn and leveled at us. "Drop that shit, kneel and put your hands on top of your heads," he said.

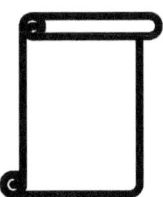

SIXTEEN

We didn't drop things; I wasn't about to risk damaging the laptop; but, we put the books and computer down as quickly as possible, and raised our hands.

"I said, get down on your knees and put your hands on top of your heads," the cop said.

His partner, the younger cop, came in behind him, his gun also drawn.

"What the hell are you two doing here?" he asked.

"We have the permission of the owner," I said. "I have the key right here in my pocket." Then I thought better of reaching for my pocket. "Or, better yet, you can call Mr.

Robert Campbell, the owner, and verify that with him."

The two exchanged glances. The young white cop, Curry something or other I recalled from before, nodded at his partner. "You keep 'em covered, I'll go call Mr. Campbell." He slipped out of the hallway.

A few minutes later, he was back. "They check out. Mr. Campbell said he gave them the key and permission to enter the place."

"Can we put our hands down now?" Buster asked.

They holstered their weapons.

"Yeah, sorry 'bout that," the black cop said. "We didn't expect anybody to be here. What are you doing here, anyway?"

"We could ask you guys the same thing. Did someone call and report prowlers or something?"

They got sheepish looks on their faces.

"Uh, I asked first." He had a stubborn set to his dark brown face.

Buster looked just as stubborn.

"Okay, I'll tell you," I said. "Despite what your boss says, we don't believe Vivienne LeClerc's death was accidental. I know we have no authority, but we were looking into it." I could have fed them our cover story about doing an insurance investigation for Campbell, but something told me that levelling with them was the best course of action.

Suddenly, they looked relieved.

"Look, could we go to the living room and sit down," the blind said. "We need to talk."

They helped us pick up the dropped books, and on the way to the living room, introduced themselves.

The young blond was Cory Lewis, age 30, who'd been a cop for five years. His partner was Derwood Williams, age 31, and he'd been on the force six years. The two of them were both natives of Lakeview, and had attended the same high school, graduating in 1989. Williams had been held back a year because of a childhood illness. They'd been on the football team together and become friends. After high school, they'd gotten a bug up their asses and joined the army together, just in time for Operation Desert Storm the following year. At the end of their three-year enlistment, they both realized that they were homesick, so, instead of reenlisting as they'd sworn they would do when they were sweating basic training together, they shucked their uniforms and returned to Lakeview, where they applied for jobs with the police department and were accepted.

Because of their shared history and apparent friendship, or just because bureaucracies work that way, they were paired up, and had been for their four years on the force, earning the nickname, the Salt and Pepper Squad.

All this tumbled out during the short walk to the living room. We dumped the books and computer on the coffee table. Lewis and Williams sat on the couch, Buster sat on the lounge chair, and I scrounged a chair from the dining room. I felt almost guilty about disturbing the sterility of the setting until I reminded myself of the condition of the bedroom. The rest of the house wasn't neat because LeClerc had been a neat person it was neat because she'd spent all her time in the bedroom, where she was, in fact, a slob.

"Okay," I said when we were settled. "You mind telling us why you two decided to do a rogue investigation of this case?"

They sat there for a long time, fiddling with their hats and avoiding eye contact. Finally, Williams, the older and obviously leader of their team, broke the silence.

"I know the chief thinks this is just an accident," he said. "File it and forget it. But, something about it don't smell right to me, to us."

"Right," Lewis said. "I can't quite put my finger on it, but my gut tells me this ain't no accident."

Buster smiled. I bit back a smile. These two had the makings of good cops, the kind who trust their gut and who are willing to think and act outside the box in the interests of justice.

"Good eyes," I said, and then explained what it was about the scene that shouted 'murder' loud and clear.

"I knew there was something that didn't

look right," Williams said. "So, what do we do now?"

"Do you have the autopsy report yet?" I asked.

"Nah, Doc Johnson said it might be ready by Wednesday. For now, he's sticking by his preliminary finding, the vic froze to death."

"Any chance of us getting a look at that report?"

They hesitated. I understood. If their chief caught them leaking information to us, it could mean their badges. I need not have worried, though.

"I think I can get him to make an extra copy," Lewis said.

"How're you gonna do that?" Buster asked.

Lewis smiled, showing a deep dimple in his left cheek. "He's my cousin," he said. "Here in Lakeview, family sticks together."

"All right, then. We'll keep you in the loop on what we uncover. Is there any way we can contact you without alerting your boss?"

Williams smiled. "Yeah, tell Bennie, one of the waiters at your hotel. He's married to my first cousin, Dorothy. Like, Cory said, here in Lakeview—"

"Family sticks together," I finished for him. *Damn, is everyone in this town related to everyone else?*

Small towns are like that, though. It's even less than six degrees of separation. You're either related to someone, or you went to school with them, which, in this case, was good for us.

We shook hands, and they left. After gathering up the recipe books and computer, Buster and I followed.

The neighborhood was as quiet as it had been when we arrived. There were a few more people outside; a white-haired gentleman playing catch with a little boy, a woman in sweats jogging on the opposite side of the street, and a couple getting into a station wagon four houses down. It looked like a perfectly normal day in any white collar suburb. The sky was bright blue with a smattering of wispy clouds. The birds were still singing their slightly off-key songs.

And, our investigation, with allies now, was beginning to take shape.

SEVENTEEN

The opening ceremony of Fantastic Fusion began with Robert Campbell, decked out in a tuxedo, going to a mike set up at the back of the dining area and introducing the mayor of Lakeview. The mayor, a portly man with a large, red nose and a white fringe of hair ringing his bulbous head, got up, and in a nasally voice welcomed the new restaurant as a new jewel in Lakeview's tourism crown. He droned on for a full ten minutes, to the point that his voice receded to the edges of my consciousness. When he finally stopped, to be replaced by a three-piece string combo playing soothing music, I took a deep breath.

"For a minute there," Sandra said. "I

thought your eyes were going to roll to the back of your head."

"Gr-r-r, you know how I hate political speeches."

"I know what you mean. I thought he'd never stop talking, but still, it's not polite to fall asleep in the middle of a speech."

I hadn't realized that my eyes were probably closed for all but his first few words. Thankfully, though, no one but Sandra noticed.

After escorting his honor, Campbell made his way to our table, a large round table with six adult chairs and two chairs that had been fitted with toddler seats, located midway between the entrance and the hastily rigged speaker's area at the back of the room. He leaned over, resting his hands on the sparkling white linen tablecloth.

"Sorry I had to put you guys through that," he said. "But, if this place is going to succeed, I have to placate the political machine."

Alma stopped trying to keep Albert and Sandra from playing with the plastic cutlery at their places at the table and looked up at him with a grin. "I never thought small towns like this had political machines," she said.

"Are you kidding me," Campbell shot back. "That's what keeps this place going. It's worse than in a big city, believe me. Here, there's no way to get away from it."

"Better you than me, bro," Buster said.

"Oh well, if things go well, the place will be set. Everyone at the head table seems to be pleased." He looked at the head table, set near the mike, where the mayor was holding forth with a group of men, decked out in tuxedos, some of them straining to hold more girth than they were designed for. Everyone was smiling. "Well, I guess I'd better go back and schmooze a bit. Got to keep the beast fed. The food will be served pretty soon, so enjoy."

He made his way back to the head table, where he was greeted with slaps on the back and handshakes.

Despite the mayor's boring speech, things seemed to be going well. I looked around the room. Everyone who was anyone in Lakeview seemed to be there. At a table near the entrance, what was in tonight's setup, the back of the room, I even saw Gavin Laine, in the company of a stunning redhead and two other couples. His gaze locked with mine. *Not everyone is happy,* I thought. The look on his face was that of a hyena that'd just been driven away from a carcass by a hungry lion. Everyone else seemed to be enjoying Campbell's apparent success; everyone, that is, but Gavin Laine.

I mentally added another name to the list of people that I wanted Heather to check up on.

Charles Ray

EIGHTEEN

The party ended at eight o'clock. This was the normal bedtime for the twins, but Alma grumbled that they'd be late going to sleep because it would take her at least an hour to clean them up. At least half the kid-sized servings of ground meat, gravy and mashed potatoes they'd been given had ended up on their faces, in their hair, and on their clothing. Campbell invited us to stay for a few celebratory drinks after everyone else had gone, but Heather begged off, saying that she had work to do. Buster and Quincy accepted, but Sandra said she needed to go for a walk to work off the rib eye she'd eaten, so we made our excuses and headed toward the lake shore.

As far north as we were, in the middle of summer, the sun doesn't fully set until well after 9:00 pm. Low in the sky, it was a dark orange ball, shooting out orange and yellow rays that pierced the pinkish clouds dotting the darkening sky. The area of the lake that we walked to was lined with trees, the east sides dark with light green highlights at their edges. The lake surface was a bronze color, like molten lava, with black shadows at the shoreline from the trees that bordered it. A gentle breeze from the north rippled the surface of the lake, creating lines of dark purple, almost black, waves.

We were alone, with nothing but the sounds of insects in the distance to keep us company. Sandra tucked her arm in mine and laid her head against my shoulder. For a moment, all else was forgotten. My world was small, just the two of us, and the warmth of her body against mine. We walked in silence for a long time.

Finally, she broke the silence. "You and Buster are investigating that woman's death, aren't you?"

She hadn't said anything about Vivienne LeClerc's death since I'd gone back to our room and told her, but I could tell it had shaken her.

"What makes you say that?"

"Come on, babe," she said. "First, I know you, and I could tell from your tone when you told me that you didn't think it was an accident. Secondly, I know you can't resist a puzzle, and this is clearly a puzzle. Finally, I recognize when Heather's doing research for you. I haven't been blind all these years, you know."

Of course, I knew she hadn't. In fact, I'd of late started taking her into my confidence and discussing cases with her, especially after the dreams stopped coming. The dreams had been disturbing, hazy images of my late wife and son, looking as they had the morning before I left for work at my job in the Pentagon, the last time I saw them alive, but I also missed them, because my conversations in those dreams often helped me make sense of some of my more difficult cases. On an intellectual level I knew that it was just my subconscious at work while I was in a dream state, but it had, while disturbing, a sense of still being in contact with them. In the last few dreams, Sarah, my late wife, had hinted that I needed to move on. Again, I knew that it was just my subconscious mind telling me what I should have already known. They were gone, and I needed to go on with my life. If I hadn't found Sandra, I'd hate to guess what state my mind would have ended up in. She was a good listener, Sandra was. A lot like Sarah in that regard, though different in every other way. She was tall, athletic, and blonde, like a Nordic goddess, with an outgoing personality, while Sarah, born in the Philippines, had been short, darker than me, with raven tresses that she always let drape to her shoulders, and except in the house, where she exerted absolute control as all Asian women do, she'd been shy almost to the point of muteness in public. What they both had in common, though, was the ability to listen and see the salient points in a complex narrative, and reduce them to simple terms, even when I was confused.

So, as we strolled along in the gathering dusk, I unloaded. I told her everything; my suspicions about the 'accident,' and why, the suspects and what I knew—which was not much—of their motives, and my concerns about the chief of police and his unexplained sudden wealth. She listened without interrupting, and when I finally reached a stopping point in my narrative, she stopped, turned and looked me squarely in the eyes.

"Al, darling," she said. "You're focusing on possible suspects, but the motives you mentioned hardly seem enough to cause someone to kill. You should be focusing on the victim."

"I know that, babe, but there's so little we know about Vivienne LeClerc."

"No, you know more than you think. In fact, the very things you *don't* know tell you a lot about her."

"Damn, you sound like Yoda in *Star Wars*. I like puzzles, but what you just said is a riddle worthy of the Sphinx."

She laughed and gently caressed the side of my face. "Okay, Grasshopper," she said. "Tell you my secrets I shall." I laughed at her weak attempt to imitate the furry little fellow's voice. "First, I saw the shoes she wore at dinner. Unless that freezer floor was slicker than an ice rink, there's no way she could have just slipped and fallen. If she was an experienced cook, she'd surely know how to navigate her way around in a freezer. If the floor was *that* slick, there's no way she would've gone into the damn thing."

"Okay, that makes sense. I actually thought much the same thing. That and the bruise on her face being on the wrong side indicated to me that she couldn't have slipped and hit her head. But, that doesn't help me determine who might've done it."

She nodded and lightly scratched the side of her nose. "True, but let's look more closely at Vivienne LeClerc herself. You say Heather's not been able to find anything on the Internet about her before she came here?"

"Right, it's like she didn't exist before coming here."

"Precisely, and that means it's likely she *didn't* exist before coming here." She tapped my chest. "At least, she didn't exist as Vivienne LeClerc. In fact, there's a good chance that Vivienne LeClerc never existed."

Light bulbs lit up in my brain. Cannons

boomed. I felt like a first-class jackass. It should've come to me before.

Whoever the dead woman in the freezer was—had been—it hadn't been a French chef named Vivienne LeClerc.

Now, I had two mysteries to solve. Who killed her, and who the hell was she.

"We've got to get back to the hotel," I said. "Right away."

"Did I give you an idea? Something useful?"

"You sure as hell did, babe. You just sent this investigation careening off in an entirely new direction."

NINETEEN

It was too late to bother either Heather or Buster by the time we got back to the spa, so I slipped notes under their doors asking them to meet me for breakfast downstairs at 7:00. For good measure, I left the same note for Quincy. Then, Sandra and I went to our suite, where I spent the next hour properly thanking her for her contribution. We drifted off to sleep around midnight, spooning, with her back to me and my arms wrapped gently around her body.

Again, if I dreamed, I don't remember it.

At 6:00 my eyes snapped open. One of the legacies of the work I did for nearly twenty years, in unnamed jungles and uncharted deserts in places that often aren't labeled on maps, is that when I wake up, I come fully awake immediately. There's no gradual transition from asleep to awake, one minute I'm sound asleep, and the next, I'm awake, alert, and aware of my surroundings. That's why I'm still around.

I looked over at Sandra, on her back with one arm thrown across her face; she was making little bubbling sounds. I debated waking her, but I had an hour before my breakfast meeting, so I eased out of bed, changed into sweats and made my way to the hotel gym, where I did a quick 30-minute workout. When I got back to the room, she was still sleeping, so I went in and took a quick shower and brushed my teeth. I decided to skip scraping the stubble, and dressed in jeans, a brown polo shirt, cotton socks and a pair of brown leather slip-ons. She was still sleeping peacefully when I left the room.

Buster was waiting for me at a table set for four when I arrived in the dining room at 6:58. Like me, he wore jeans, but with a Washington Redskins sweatshirt with the sleeves cut out. I hate the team, but he's been a lifelong fan, so I cut him some slack. On occasion, I wore a Dallas Cowboy shirt just to piss him off.

"How'd you know there'd only be four of us?" I asked.

"Alma said we had a late night last night, she was on vacation, and if I didn't get the hell out of the room and let her and the kids sleep she'd hire a divorce lawyer if she didn't kill me first. I figured Sandra would feel pretty much the same."

I had to laugh at that. "Yeah, she was still sawing logs when I left the room."

"So, we let 'em sleep. Should we get breakfast?"

"Let's just get coffee and wait for Quince and Heather."

He signaled for the waiter, a slightly built young Hispanic and ordered a pot of coffee and four cups. The man had a large urn of coffee and the requested containers within two minutes.

We were halfway through our first cup when Quincy and Heather entered the restaurant, saw us and came over. Heather was carrying her laptop and notepad, and wearing knee-length khaki shorts and a blue and pink polka dot shirt, while Quincy wore a pair of blue dress slacks and a beige short sleeve shirt open at the collar—his way of being casual. They sat and Quincy poured himself a cup of coffee. Heather waved the waiter over.

"Yes, ma'am," the young man said with a strong Spanish accent. "How may I help you?"

"Do you have tea?"

"*Si*, what kind would you like?"

Her eyes went round. "You have more than one kind?"

"*Si senorita*," he said. "We have about ten

varieties, what type would you like?"

"Do you have oolong?"

"*Claro*, would you like light, dark, or spicy dark?"

She clapped her hands, with a wide smile that showed all her teeth. "I'll have the light, please."

"*Uno momento, senorita.*" He walked toward the bar, near which was a long table with several teapots and boxes of tea.

"Wow," she said. "I could get used to this."

A few minutes later, the waiter returned with a pot from which steam rose in a thin line and a small porcelain cup.

"Would the *senorita* like tea or lemon with her tea?"

"No, this if fine, *muchas gracias.*"

She poured a cup, blew on it and took a sip. She sat back and sighed deeply.

"Now, that's the way to start the day. Okay, boss, do we do business first, or do we eat first?" She pointed at the buffet line.

"We get our food, and we work while we eat," I said.

A few minutes later we were back at the table. Buster and I had our plates loaded pretty much to overflowing with everything from the line except oatmeal or dry cereal. Quincy had an egg over medium, hashed browns, two slices of bacon and two slices of whole wheat toast, and Heather had a bowl of corn flakes, a single piece of rye toast with a pat of grape jam, and four grapes from the fruit basket. I can't speak for Buster, who I suspect just likes to eat—a holdover from his football playing days perhaps—but I was taught that breakfast is the most important meal of the day, and if you're going to overeat, that's the meal to do it, because as the day progresses you'll burn off the excess calories. It worked for me when I was younger. Of course, over fifty now, and with a slower metabolism, I *was* beginning to get a bit soft around the middle, but I'd wrestled with myself over whether to trim the breakfast or just exercise more. Exercising more won out, especially now that Sandra liked to exercise with me.

The one thing I kept to a bare minimum was dry cereal. Oh, I know, the food ads and the government pound your skull with the information that cereals are good for you, but I beg to differ. The next time you're in the store, take a moment and read the ingredients label on your favorite cereal. Chances are sugar is one of the ingredients listed second or third, and if not, I'll bet you that wheat or wheat flour is one of the main ingredients, no matter what the front of the box claims it to be. And, my friend, if you think eating a lot of wheat is good for you I've got a plot of land in the Arizona desert with your name on it. The wheat we eat today resembles its ancient ancestor about as much as the space shuttle resembles a kite. Over the centuries, farmers have adapted and bred the modest wheat plant in order to get better yields to the point that it's almost a different plant entirely. Wheat, unfortunately, is the main source of gluten, a kind of protein in wheat and other grains that is what helps grain flour stick together. It has almost zero nutritional value, and acts on the stomach lining and colon in ways that lead to all kinds of stomach or intestinal diseases, and also, because it knocks your blood sugar out of whack, is one of the main sources of belly fat, which, believe me, is a lot more dangerous than that double chin you worry about because it's a hell of a lot harder to get rid of. So, if you ever wondered why Americans and other people who eat lots of bread are so damned fat, don't blame beer, blame bread made from wheat, rye, oat, and other grains. I like the occasional piece of toast, love biscuits with jam or gravy, and can't imagine eating fried chicken or pork shops without cornbread, but I try to avoid a breakfast that's just toast and cereal if I can because, drum roll please, it's just too unhealthy.

I would never tell Heather that, though. She'd just look at me down that beautiful turned up nose of hers and remind me of how much cholesterol went down my gullet on any given day. I guess everyone has to decide on his or her own poison. I copied Buster, and began to dig into my pile of food.

When the pile had a significant dent in it, and my morning hunger pangs were, if not assuaged, at least temporarily placated, I leaned back and took a sip of coffee.

"Okay, you guys keep eating, and I'll summarize what we know so far," I said.

I did, and it didn't take long. We didn't know all that much. It did start a lively discussion, though.

"I think I agree with Sandra," Quincy said. "Vivienne LeClerc sounds fishy. I mean, who doesn't have at least *some* kind of record somewhere? If she was supposed to be some kind of fancy chef, it doesn't make sense."

I lifted my coffee cup in a toast.

"Good point, Quince. Heather, what've you gotten off her laptop that might shed some light on her?"

"Bupkis," she said. "The damn thing's password-protected. I haven't been able to get past the log-in screen."

"Hey, I thought you were the computer whiz who could make the damn machines stand up and dance. Why can't you just go into whatever file that has the password and extract it or something?" I'd picked up a lot of computer jargon from Heather over the years, even though I hadn't the faintest idea what most of it meant, or what I'd just said, and that was obvious from the look she gave me.

"Because, oh Great One," she said, ice dripping from each word. "I need the password in order to get into the directory that contains the password."

"Oh, that's a bummer. I'll bet she has stuff

on that computer of hers that would help identify her."

She sniffed. 'Sn-f'. "You think? Anyway, it's not totally hopeless. After breakfast, I'll go back up and work on it some more." She shot me a stony glare. "I *will* crack it."

"Okay, anything else," I said, hoping that I was steering the conversation to safer ground.

Her expression brightened. "As a matter of fact, yes. There's more on our friend, Samuel Holiday. I'm not sure what it means, but it's interesting." She put her teacup down and flipped open her notepad, riffling pages until she came to the one she wanted. "Ah, here it is. I found references to the property and car, cars actually, since his wife has a new Mercedes 500SL, associated with Samuel Holiday, but upon a deeper dive into the files I found something interesting." She paused. "None of it, including the car he personally drives, is in his name. It's all in his wife's name."

That caused everyone to stop eating, forks, or in my case coffee cup, frozen in midair. "That is a bit unusual. What's the story there?"

"The current wife's name is Lanya, Lanya Perestrovka. Apparently, she was a mail-order bride of sorts. Holiday met her through one of those dating services that hook American men up with Russian women looking for husbands. It's been a growth industry since the Soviet Union collapsed."

"How long have they been married?"

"According to the news reports I found, they got married in 2001, so just a bit over two years."

This was getting more and more interesting. "So, the chief dumps his first wife, marries a Russian, and then puts everything in her name. What've you got on the first wife?"

"Nothing yet, but I'm working on it."

Quincy and Buster were sitting quietly, their attention shifting from me to Heather and back like spectators at a tennis match. Quincy finally broke the silence.

"I'll bet you anything, he's done that to keep from having to share his assets with the former wife," he said.

"That's gotta piss her off," Buster said.

I smiled. Another possible ally, perhaps? "And, if she's pissed off, she might just be willing to share whatever dirt she has on her ex. Heather, along with getting into LeClerc's computer, make finding Holiday's ex-wife a priority. What else you got?"

"Just the background information on the people at Fantastic Fusions. Do you want the long or short version?"

I told her to decide for herself what we needed to know to move forward. What she gave lay somewhere between long and short, and filled in a few of the blank spaces in my mind.

She started with Robert Campbell, darting occasional glances at Buster as she spoke. There was not much there, really. What she'd found pretty much jibed with what Buster had already told us. Campbell came from a wealthy family, not inherited wealth; his father had made a few good real estate investments and parlayed them into millions, all of which came to Campbell, the only child, when his parents died within months of each other, the mother from pancreatic cancer, and the father probably from just not wanting to live without her. Campbell, who had playing defensive halfback for the Denver Broncos at the time, took time off from playing to attend each funeral, left the family fortune to grow in the bank accounts and stocks his father had invested in, and when his knees started giving him trouble eighteen months earlier, had turned in his jersey and returned home to try his hand at business. He was, thanks to his father's estate, the sole owner of the spa and dozens of other lucrative residential and commercial properties scattered around Chautauqua County, but mostly in and around Lakeview, and had a few months earlier announced his plans to open Fantastic Fusions to give locals and tourists more dining choices.

Next up was the waiter, Sanjay Guptar, who had found the body. Born in Bombay, now Mumbai, India, he'd immigrated to the United States with his parents when he was eighteen. He was now forty, and had moved from New York City, where his family settled to be near his father's younger brother, a computer engineer, after his mother died two years earlier. His father and uncle, as far as Heather could determine, still lived in the city. Guptar was unmarried and lived alone in a small cottage on the eastern edge of Lakeview. He had no criminal record, and his work history indicated that he'd worked as a waiter since coming to Lakeview, first for Gavin Laine, and then at the spa, until Campbell moved him to the new restaurant.

Jerome Collins, the young waiter, was a native of Lakeview. After graduating from high school, he'd gone to a community college in Buffalo, and returned home after graduation. Like Guptar, he'd worked at the spa, but as a pool boy, until Campbell hired him for the restaurant. He lived with his parents in one of Lakeview's working class neighborhoods.

Sunyi Kim had lived with her parents in Pittsburgh, Pennsylvania before coming to Lakeview three years earlier. Like Collins, she'd been part of the spa wait staff, and had been hired by Campbell for the new restaurant. She lived in a rooming house on the north side of town, just inside the city limits. She had no criminal record, and no known relationships outside work.

Jefferson Aldercott was a freelance accountant who kept the books for several of the town's smaller businesses. He worked from his home, a modest-sized, modest-priced ranch style house in one of the up and coming middle class neighborhoods. Married, with two kids, he was active in the local Presbyterian Church as a lay deacon.

Walter Muncie, Campbell's sous chef, and our main suspect, was also single. In his mid-thirties, he lived alone in a tiny box-shaped house a few miles from the lake spa complex, even though his parents still lived in town, in a working class neighborhood not far from where the Collins family lived. Muncie had gone to New York City, where he completed a course at a fly-by-night school of 'culinary arts,' and returned to Lakeview after working at several fry cook jobs in the Big Apple. He'd worked as a junior cook in the spa's kitchen until Campbell hired him to be Fantastic Fusion's sous chef.

That was all she had, and it didn't shed any further light on who would want to see Vivienne LeClerc dead. My disappointment must have shown on my face.

"Sorry, Al, but that's all I could come up with in 24 hours," she said. She looked crestfallen. For Heather, any hint that she wasn't up to the task hit hard.

"Hey, for the short time you had, you did a damn good job," I said. "It's just that we don't know anything so far that helps us solve this case." Her face fell farther. "But, if you can get into LeClerc's computer, I feel sure you'll find something that'll be helpful."

She smiled. "I think you're right. As soon as I finish my breakfast, I'll get on that."

I felt pretty confident she'd do it, too.

She finished off her breakfast pretty quickly, made her excuses, and left. Quincy, Buster and I took a few more minutes to polish ours off, although, Quincy just slowed his eating to avoid finishing ahead of us. Finally, we were sitting there, looking at our empty plates and sipping our second cups of coffee.

"Okay," Quincy said. "I know it'd do no good for me to tell you two to let this thing drop. Neither of you have any jurisdiction up here in New York, you're skating very close to the edge of the law by pursuing this investigation, and could get into some serious trouble if the chief of police decided to push. But I also know that the two of you make mules seem reasonable, and nothing I say will dissuade you. So, what do we do next?"

"I thought you said we could get in trouble for pursuing an investigation outside our jurisdiction?" I said.

"Unlike the two of you, I don't have that problem. In addition to the DC, Maryland, and Virginia bars, I'm also a member in good standing of the New York bar association. So, when you get yourselves arrested, I'll be able to legally represent you."

"I'm not sure I can afford you," Buster said.

"Don't worry." Quincy laughed. "I'll just take my fees from Al's retainer."

I'm pretty sure he wasn't joking about that, unless it was some kind of lawyer humor, but it was good to know he had our backs, even if we did have to pay for the privilege.

"Okay, good to know," I said. "Buster, I think our next step would be to talk to your friend again."

"I thought you agreed he wasn't really a suspect?"

"I don't mean talk to him as a suspect. I want to know what he knows about the interpersonal dynamics among his staff. I got a gut feeling that one or more of them was less than candid with us."

That placated him. "Yeah, they're all hiding something if you ask me. Let's roll."

We were just stepping off the bottom step outside when a Lakeview Police car rolled to a stop in front of us. The driver, hair in coiled braids with skin the color of polished mahogany, was large, not fat, but amply proportioned, with not a lot of clearance between her breasts and the steering wheel. The window on the driver's side was open, and the expression on her dark brown face was anything but friendly as she looked at us. We started to walk around the vehicle.

'Hold up, gentlemen," she said. Her voice was deep, resonant, and commanding. "The chief would like a word with you."

That was when I noticed Samuel Holiday sitting in the back seat. What kind of police chief has himself chauffeured around like that, I thought. Well, a pompous, fat ass loser like this, of course. I stopped walking; Buster and Quincy moved in to flank me.

Slowly, and somewhat ponderously, Holiday hauled his bulk out of the back seat. His belly jiggled as he adjusted his gun belt. He straightened his hat, brushed at the stars on his collars and glared at us.

"I thought I made myself clear to you gentlemen," he said. "You were not to conduct an investigation into the death of Vivienne LeClerc in my town."

"You did," I said. "And, we're not." The lie fell easily from my lips. I prefer the truth, but with slugs like Holiday, all bets are off.

"Then, what were you doing at her house?"

Shit, did one of those young cops rat on us? "How do you know we were at LeClerc's place of residence?"

"I have my sources."

Good. If it'd been one of them, no reason he wouldn't tell us. It's a small town. Maybe one of the neighbors saw us and reported it.

"Okay, we were there, but that doesn't make an investigation."

"You were trespassing," he said. "I could run you in for that."

Quincy stepped forward. "They were in the house with the permission of the owner," he said. "He gave them a key."

"And, you are?" Holiday's voice dripped with sarcasm.

Quincy regarded him levelly. "I am Quincy Chang, attorney-at-law, and I represent Mr. Pennyback and Detective Mayweather." I could imagine him skewering some witness in the courtroom with that perfectly modulated voice.

Holiday didn't seem impressed. "Well, Mr. Quincy Chang, are you licensed to practice law in the great state of New York?"

"As a matter of fact, I am. Would you like my bar association membership number? I can give you the phone number of the bar association in Albany if you wish to check."

A flicker of doubt, a glimmer of hesitation flashed across Holiday's fat, florid face. "Uh, that won't be necessary. Just make sure your . . . clients don't break any laws in my town."

He turned and levered himself back into the car. The busty cop driving smiled up at me, tilting her head a fraction of an inch, and drove away. Holiday wasn't a very popular man among his troops.

As the car pulled out of the parking lot, Quincy let out a big sigh. "Whew!" He wiped his brow.

"Uh, Quince," I said. "Don't tell me that you were just bluffing with the man about being a member of the New York bar?"

He looked at me with a lopsided grin on his face. "Okay, I won't tell you."

Buster chuckled. "Looks like he's been hanging 'round with you a bit too long."

We all laughed at that. I've never thought of myself as a corrupting influence. I try to follow the rules, until they get in the way of getting the job done. But, when I do break the rules, I at least try my level best not to hurt anyone—anyone innocent, that is. I don't lose any sleep when the guilty are collateral damage, because they put themselves in harm's way by doing bad things.

We found Robert Campbell in his office. He was seated behind his desk peering intently at a large spreadsheet. He looked up and smiled when we entered.

"Hey, guys, what's shaking? Nice opening, except for the mayor's speech." He stabbed a finger on the spreadsheet. "And, we're already booked solid through the end of the month."

"So, Muncie's working out as head chef?" I asked.

He frowned. "He's okay . . . but, I'm not sure he has the chops to be a head chef. Walter's a competent craftsman, but a head chef also has to have a certain . . . *panache*, and he just doesn't have it."

"He's not gonna be a happy camper to be promoted, and then demoted, you know that, right? I mean, he had to have resented you bringing Vivienne in from the outside . . . now, if you bring in another, you just might lose him."

"Damn, I'd hate to lose him. He's a townie, and one of the things I wanted to do, as much as I possibly could, was involve the locals. But, it also has to be a successful business, which means I have to make hard personnel decisions. One of those decisions is that Walter Muncie is just not head chef material."

This guy approached business like he played football. You had to focus on the goal, move the ball forward, get a first down, get some more first downs, and win the game. You work with your teammates, but if a teammate is not holding up his end of the line, you pull him out of the game. Nothing personal, just business. I understood it on an intellectual level, but I could also see it from Walter Muncie's perspective. He was being screwed. Not deliberately, or maliciously, but screwed nonetheless. That could drive some people to do desperate things, even murder. Had it driven him? If it did, what might it do to him when Campbell announced that he'd be getting yet another head chef and bumping Walter back down to the sous chef position?

More questions for which I had no answer.

"Better you than me, I suppose," I said. "By the way, have you been able to get through to LeClerc's next of kin about disposition of the remains."

"Funny that you should bring that up." He rubbed at his cheek. "The number Vivienne gave me has been disconnected for the past six months. I even tried directory assistance, but they don't have a listing."

I hadn't shared with him our belief that Vivienne LeClerc might be an assumed identity. When I did, he just sat there with his mouth open for a few seconds.

"Shit," was all he said.

Shit, there wasn't much else *to* say.

We'd given him back the key to LeClerc's place, but I had a feeling that we needed to take another look around, so I asked for it back.

"You going there, now?" he asked.

"Yeah, but first I have to talk to someone. I'll keep you in the loop if we find anything."

He handed over the key, and Buster and I left.

"Who we gonna talk to?" Buster asked as we left the restaurant.

"Our two young cop friends," I said.

"About what?"

"Trust."

Charles Ray

TWENTY

We walked back to the spa. In the dining room, we found Benito Suarez in the area near the kitchen. He was sorting menus and stacking them neatly on a table near the door. He looked up and smiled as we approached.

"*Buenos Dias, senores*, how are you today?"

"We're fine, Bennie," I said.

"What can I do for you?" He put the menu he was holding down and turned to face us.

"I need to speak with your cousin."

Without hesitation, he pulled out his cell phone. "Is it of urgency?"

"Yeah, you could say that. I have to ask him something."

He hit speed dial. "May I tell him what it

is?" He held the phone to his ear as he spoke.

"I'd rather ask him in person, if you don't mind. Can you arrange for him to meet us somewhere . . . private?"

"*Si, claro, uno momento.* Derwood," he said into the phone. "*Si*, it is Bennie. Your . . . new friend wishes a private meeting with you."

"And, his partner too," I said.

"He also wishes to speak with Cory. Yes, it is private, and he says it is important." He listened for a few seconds. "*Si*, I will tell him."

He broke the connection and put the phone back into the pocket of his pants. "He will meet with you in twenty minutes." He gave us directions to a little park on the lake about three miles south of town, and went back to sorting his menus.

We took my car. The park was easy to find, a small white sign with green borders identified it. We arrived with five minutes to spare and I parked in a space back from the street. Three minutes later, a Lakeview police cruiser pulled in next to us. Lewis was driving. He and his partner, Williams, got out and walked to the driver's side of my car. We got out and joined them, standing near the front.

"Hey, Mr. Pennyback, Detective Mayweather," Lewis said. Williams smiled and saluted us by touching his index finger to the brim of his cap. "Bennie said it was important."

"It is," I said.

He motioned to a copse of small trees at the back of the park, behind a picnic table. "Maybe we should walk over there," he said. "Might not be such a good idea being seen talking to you two in public."

Buster and I followed them to a little clearing behind the trees.

"What's so urgent?" Williams asked.

"I got a visit from your chief this morning," I said. "He knew that we were at the LeClerc place."

They weren't smiling now.

"Yeah," Williams said. "We know. We got our asses reamed this morning, probably right after he talked to you."

"So, you didn't tell him we were there?"

The looks of shock on their faces came too suddenly and were too sincere to be faked.

"No, no way," Lewis said. "If he thought we were working with you, it'd mean our badges. We just told him we'd come up on you there."

"And, we only told him that because he asked what we were doing there with you," Williams added. "We said we were doing a routine patrol in the area and saw the car in the driveway. We knew that was the dead woman's house, so we worried it might be a prowler, so we checked. Since you guys had the key, we figured it was okay, so we left."

"Do you know how he knew that you were there?"

Their heads shook in unison. "I figure some neighbor must've called the chief,"

Williams said. "This is a small town, and like most small towns, it has more than its share of nosy people."

Their account sounded sincere. Our team was still intact, for the moment. But, what I planned to do next put it at risk.

"We're going back for another look," I said.

"Uh, you sure that's a good idea?" Williams looked dubious.

"I think this time we'll park somewhere other than the driveway, and go on foot. Hopefully, no one will notice. I didn't see too many people on the streets last time we were there."

They looked at each other. Finally, Williams smiled. "I have an idea. Maybe we can help. People notice any time a police car's in the area, so if we drive into the area, a block or two away from the house, and you approach from the opposite direction, everyone'll be looking at us and not notice you."

I had to laugh. It was so simple, it just might work, and the two of them were really taking to the cloak and dagger stuff. "Okay. Do you two have time to do it right now?"

They nodded. "Sure," he said. "Give us a couple of minutes and then follow. We'll take a back street and come into the neighborhood from the north. You should park at least a block or two south and walk up. If you use the service road in back of the house, you're not likely to be seen."

"But, the key's for the front door."

"No problem," Lewis said. "If it's like most of the houses here, the front and back lock use the same key."

It didn't sound like very practical home security, but I suppose it beat having to carry a bunch of keys around all the time. I nodded, and they went back to their car and quickly pulled out of the park, heading back toward town. Buster and I gave them three minutes and followed.

I parked the Volkswagen in front of a house with a 'For Sale' sign on the lawn, about a block and a half from LeClerc's place. Buster and I got out and made our way across the yard and behind to the service road used by the sanitation department's trash pickup trucks. It didn't take long to reach the house. We didn't see anyone, and hopefully, no one saw us.

Some of the homes had fenced in back yards. Fortunately, the house LeClerc had rented didn't, and also fortunately, Lewis had been right, the key slid in and the door opened.

Except for a cabinet door slightly ajar, the kitchen looked the same as it had before. We started through, but a niggling thought at the back of my mind caused me to stop and go back to that cabinet over the sink. I opened the door fully and looked inside. As I did, I pulled up a mental image of what it had looked like when I peered inside during our first visit. The image didn't quite mesh up with what I was seeing now. A couple of items seemed to be slightly out of position. I felt an itchy sensation at the base of my skull.

"Let's check the bedroom," I said.

Buster followed me through the living room, down the hallway, and into the pigsty that was the late Vivienne LeClerc's bedroom. We stopped just inside the door.

When you're conducting reconnaissance, even if it's an area that you've been to before, it's a good idea to get the general lay of the land and compare it with what you remember, before proceeding further. The little inconsistencies I'd noticed with the items in the pantry gave me the feeling that all was not as it should be. I held up a hand to keep Buster from entering, and scanned the room from right to left, left to right, starting with the area nearest me and working to the farthest wall.

Sure enough, there were signs that some had been there since our last visit. It wasn't anything glaringly obvious like footprints, but to me it was as clear as a big neon sign. Near the closet, a blue sweater that had been in a crumpled ball was now more flattened out, a shoe that sat at the end of the bed was now on its side, and the rumpled blanket had been pulled an inch further down toward the foot of the bed. Someone had, since we were there, come in and searched the room. I imagined, among the things they were looking for, the laptop computer I'd removed and given to Heather was at the top of their list, if they'd known it was there.

I tensed up.

"What's wrong?" Buster asked.

"Can't you see, someone's been here."

"Huh?" He looked around. His brows scrunched up and looked like two caterpillars trying to reach each other. "How can you tell?"

Buster's a good detective. But, the signs I saw were, I suppose, a bit too subtle for him. They were, after all, almost microscopic, the kinds of things the average person takes no notice of, like a leaf not hanging properly on a branch, or a twig of grass slightly bent because someone passing stopped and rested their weight against it for a few seconds. These are the types of things that missing can get you killed on a mission in hostile territory. I explained what I'd seen in the kitchen, and what I was seeing now, looking at the, to him, clutter of the bedroom.

"It looks like someone was looking for something."

"How you can tell that in all this mess I don't know, but I'll take your word for it, Sherlock. Who do you think it was, and what were they looking for?"

"I wish I knew who," I said. "As to what, for starters, I'd imagine they'd love to get their hands on her computer."

The import of what I'd said hit us both at

the same time. I reacted first, spinning and heading out of the bedroom and down the hall toward the kitchen and out the back door.

I'd given Heather the computer, and she was alone in her hotel room.

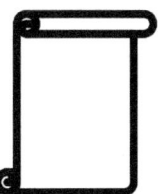

TWENTY-ONE

I probably broke every traffic law on Lakeview's books getting back to the spa. After I'd parked as close to the building as I could, Buster and I jumped out of the car and sprinted across the parking lot, through the lobby, and, ignoring the elevator, up the stairs to the third floor where Heather's room was. We were both a bit winded when we came out of the stairwell, so I held up a hand for us to halt, catch our breath, and assess the situation.

The hallway was empty. Heather's room was near the elevator, about midway down the hall from the stairwell door. Not the ideal place to be in the event of a fire or some other emergency requiring evacuation, but the place was booked solid, and we'd only gotten rooms because we were guests of the owner.

After our breathing had returned to normal, we began to move slowly toward Heather's room.

I'm not given to fantasizing about things; to imagining the worse when faced with an unknown situation. I also don't imagine that everything unknown is fine. Like Schroedinger's Cat, which is both alive and dead until the box is opened and we know for sure, a situation just is until we have the details. But, I always prepare for the worse. The situation might be neutral, in which case your preparations aren't necessary, it might be positive, making them silly perhaps, but it might be nasty, in which case . . . better to have prepared and not need it than need it and not be prepared.

We reached her door without seeing or hearing anything in the hallway. I put my ear to the door. Through the thin wood, I could hear the hum of the room air conditioner and the muffled sound of music. Heather liked to listen to music when she worked on the computer. I rapped on the door. When it started to swing inwards, I tensed, just in case, but it was just Heather standing there, in cutoff jeans and a yellow tee shirt with a big red heart on the front and a number two yellow pencil poking out of her mussed blonde mop just over her left ear.

"Hey, Al, Buster, come on in." She stepped aside. "I was just about to call you guys."

We looked at each other with expressions of relief as we stepped inside.

Heather didn't have a suite like Buster and me, but the room she was in was still huge. A king-sized bed sat in the center, with a large flat screen TV mounted on the wall opposite the foot. To the right of the entrance was the bathroom, with a walk-in tub and shower, and to the left was a counter with a mini-fridge, a separate, well-stocked mini-bar, a microwave, and a complete set of cooking utensils, cutlery, and flatware. A desk sat against the wall to the right of the TV, and the entire far wall was composed of glass sliding doors that led onto a balcony with a small round table and two chairs where the room occupant could sit and enjoy the view of Chautauqua Lake.

Heather had her laptop and LeClerc's laptop side by side on the desk, along with a couple of notepads. Both were open, and the exposed pages covered in her neat handwriting. On the floor next to the chair, the books we'd taken from LeClerc's closet lay scattered.

"Looks like you've been busy," I said. "What were you gonna call us about?"

She sat at the desk, and motioned Buster to the lounge chair opposite the desk in the corner and me to the foot of the bed.

"This woman had some serious security on her computer," she said. "But, like most people, she was lazy, or forgetful, so she was careless with her password."

"Damn," Buster said. "You figured out her password?"

"More like found it. People have a tendency to come up with easy passwords, like their spouse's birthdate or a favorite pet's name, which hackers can suss out in minutes, or they create a hard-to-figure password and have to write it down somewhere because they're likely to forget it. In this case it was a combination of the two." She leaned and picked up a book of salad recipes that had been splayed face down on the floor. "Her password was simplicity itself, but I might never have guessed it, because it required knowing things about her I didn't know. For some reason, though, she wrote it down."

She turned the book around and flipped to the back page. On the inside back cover was written, 'coralgables'.

"What caused you to look through the books?" I asked.

"It was just a hunch. I didn't know enough about her to try guessing at her password. Besides, like I said, most people are lazy, and write their password down somewhere. I'll give her credit, though; a lot of hackers might not have thought to look in recipe books for a password. Anyway, I started flipping through the books, and saw 'coralgables' on the fourth book."

"How'd you know it was a password?" Buster, who is only marginally more computer literate than me, asked.

"Come on, it's obvious. All lowercase letters and no spacing. Anyway, I typed it in and *voila*, I was in. I've been going through her files for the past two hours."

Something Heather had said triggered a thought in my mind. "You said some people chose a password related to something in their lives; does 'coralgables' mean something special here?"

She smiled and gave me one of her 'you're turning into a capable student' looks. "It does, but not in the way you'd think. I thought at first it might be because she was from Florida, and I wasted half an hour trying to locate her focusing on Coral Gables, Florida and surrounding areas, but it was a bust."

"So, what is the significance, then?"

"Another thing people do is use names for passwords, and that's what our girl did in this case. When I did a search focusing on 'coralgables' as a name, bingo, I found her." She picked up one of the notepads and flipped it open. "I started a search using 'Coral Gables,' but came up with nothing. Then, I tried Cora L. Gables, and there she was; Cora Lee Gables of Topeka, Kansas, not Vivienne LeClerc, and certainly not French."

"You sure it was her?"

"Oh, I'm sure. One of her classmates at Seminole High School was appointed to the Air Force Academy, and the local paper did a big spread on it, including pictures of him and a lot of his classmates. Little Miss Cora Lee Gable, was a cheerleader, and featured prominently in several of the pictures. Except for a change in hair color, she hadn't changed much since high school. There's no doubt about it, Vivienne LeClerc is, was, Cora Lee Gables."

"Now, that certainly puts this whole case in a different light," I said. "If Vivienne LeClerc is an alias, what the hell was Cora Lee Gables up to?"

"It gets even better, or worse depending on your point of view." She flipped a couple more pages of the notebook. "Our friend Cora Lee has an arrest record as long as my arm, mostly for running con games. She was convicted once, and served two years in the state pen in Illinois. On the others there was never enough evidence to convict, or the marks dropped charges. Ms. Gables has been a ba-a-a-ad girl," Heather said with a smirk on her elfin face.

"Damn, it don't sound like Bob did any kind of background check on this woman," Buster said.

"Before we judge him too harshly, why don't you call him and ask him to bring us everything he has on her," I said. "It could just be she had papers that looked good. From the sound of what Heather's dug up, this woman's an experienced grifter."

He grumbled, but took out his phone and called Campbell. After telling him what we wanted, he kept his ear to the phone for a while, then broke the connection and put it back into his pocket. "He'll be up in about five minutes," he said.

"Okay, Heather, do you have anything else for us?"

"Well, I did like you said and put most of my effort into Vivienne, er, I mean, Cora's computer," she said. "It was mostly recipes. Looks like she was doing a lot of late night studying to pull off her impersonation of a chef. I got into her email account. Not a lot there; which is no surprise. She probably didn't have a lot of friends. There were two emails, though, that struck me as strange."

"What was strange about them?"

She opened Gables' computer. When she brushed the space bar, the screen lit up, blinked, and settled on an AOL email inbox. She used a mouse she'd attached to the machine to highlight the incoming emails, and then spaced down to one near the bottom of the screen and clicked on it. The screen blinked and an email filled it.

GEL gel69@hotmail.com   *July 1*
    To: Gabby@aol.com
Cora, I don't know what you're up to, but I know

who you are.

Meet me tonight at 10:30 at the Oak Tavern on Lake Street.

So, Vivienne/Cora must be Gabby, I figured, but who the hell was GEL, and why was he or she demanding a meeting with her six days before she died? "Any idea where that email came from?" I asked.

"No. It could have come from anywhere, but from the language, I'd guess it was someone from the area. It gets better though." She skipped down, which loaded a new page of emails. Three down from the top, she opened another.

GEL gel69@hotmail.com   *July 5*
    To: Gabby@aol.com
   I hope you've given my offer some thought. It's not renewable.

I didn't like the tone of that email. It could be taken as a threat, or at a minimum, an ultimatum. Given that this was the day before she died, my money was on it being a threat.

"Heather," I said. "You have a new priority task. Find out who the hell GEL is. I think we just got ourselves a new suspect."

"I'm on it, but it's gonna take some time. These email providers don't just hand out information like that without a court order . . . which I doubt we can get."

"You trying to tell me it's impossible?"

"No, I'm *telling* you it'll take me some time. This will have to be done delicately. It's not like I can just go up and bust open a safe or something. I have to get past who knows how many firewalls and other protective measures, and then sift through millions of bits and bytes, so keep your shirt on."

Her voice had a little bite in it. Heather doesn't like her ability doubted, and she doesn't like being rushed or crowded. I raised my hands in mock surrender. "Sorry, I wasn't trying to rush you, and by no means was I doubting your ability. I just wanted to be sure."

My apology was sincere, it was heartfelt. No way was I about to alienate the brains of the company. She didn't smile, but the softening of her expression told me I was off the hook—for now.

The tinny bell announced that someone was at the door. I hopped up and went and opened it. Campbell stood there with a thick manila folder under his arm and a puzzled expression on his face.

"I brought Vivienne's file like Buster requested," he said, handing the folder to me. "What's all this about?"

I had him sit on the foot of the bed, and while I thumbed through the folder, I filled him on what we, mainly Heather, had found. His puzzled expression changed to shock, and then anger.

"So, you see," I said. "Vivienne LeClerc doesn't exist except on the phony papers Cora Gables presented to you."

"Damn, I can't believe she played me like that. What the hell was she trying to get out of it? I can't see how her being a cook in my restaurant would get her much in the way of money."

"Didn't you do a background check on her?" Buster asked.

Campbell looked at him, his eyebrows raised. "Background check? We're not talking about a top secret project here, just a restaurant. I checked the references she gave me, and they came back okay."

Depending upon where those references purported to come from, I had no doubt they did. If Gables was even a half-assed grifter, she would've made sure that any papers she gave her mark were backstopped. I needed to know the answer to one question to validate my theory that Campbell was indeed her intended mark.

"How'd you find LeClerc?" I asked.

"I put an ad for a chef in a couple of New York City papers. She contacted me, first by email, and then, because she painted a good picture in her email, I asked for, and she mailed me her work reference. I called the two restaurants she claimed to have worked for in New York, and they gave her glowing recommendations. Her resume said she studied at some school in France, which closed its doors six years ago. I looked it up on the Internet, and that checked out. I had her come here and cook a meal for me—the woman was a good cook. What more was there to know?"

The look on Campbell's face told it all. He had, in fact, done what any reasonable employer would have done, but he'd been had. That had to hurt. Buster looked down at his feet. I felt bad for them both, but there was no time for emotional healing at this point. We had a dead woman, a killer out there somewhere, and a local cop who didn't seem interested in doing anything but keeping us from getting at the truth.

"Look," I said. "No one can blame you. This woman was an experienced grifter. It's likely she had someone manning the phone numbers she'd given you who backed up her story."

"I suppose you're right, but that still leaves the question of why she targeted me and my restaurant in the first place."

"I have a feeling that if we figure that out, we might just figure out who killed her."

He leaned forward with his elbows on his thighs and his head cupped in his hands. "Damn, this is getting stranger and stranger."

"It's not helped by your chief of police threatening to run us out of town if we keep investigating."

He sat up, a frown on his face. "Sam Holiday is an incompetent blowhard, but he was supportive of the restaurant. I should be able to convince him to stay off your backs."

Somehow I doubted that. Incompetent, no doubt. A blowhard, looked that way. But, he seemed adamant about Buster and me not digging into the case, and I had a feeling Campbell's money and family background wouldn't help much. In fact, if Campbell went to him, he'd know that we'd lied about our activities from the get-go.

"Hold off on that for now," I said. "We're working a few angles, and I think we might have it under control."

I had my fingers crossed behind my back.

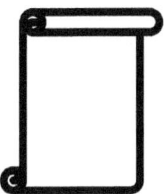

TWENTY–TWO

The rest of the day drifted by like the clouds that drifted slowly across the blue sky or the ducks that floated lazily on the lake. Until Heather came up with more details, there wasn't much investigating Buster and I could do. All of us got together early for dinner so the twins could join us, and then everyone retired to their respective rooms.

Sandra and I sat on the balcony until well after 10:00, enjoying the soft breeze blowing down from the north, and listening to the sounds of the night birds, and then we showered together, left our clothing scattered from the bathroom to the bed, and finally, around 12:45, we fell asleep in a tangle of limbs.

We were up at 7:00 the next morning, and after brushing our teeth to get rid or morning breath, we spent thirty minutes in the spa's gym. Another couple was there, and initially tried to link up with us, but when they saw how Sandra and I sparred, decided to leave us alone, and shortly thereafter, left the gym.

After working up a good sweat, we went back to the room, showered, dressed, and by 8:00 were seated at a large round table in the dining room, with full plates in front of us.

The rest of our crew filtered down from their rooms by 8:25; Heather first, still looking mopey because she'd found nothing new to aid our investigation, Quincy, looking dapper in khaki shorts and a Hawaiian shirt, and finally, Buster and his brood. After getting food, and getting the twins somewhat settled in toddler chairs, we ate in as much silence as can be managed with two active toddlers trying to see how much of their food they could get on their clothing, and Alma trying to keep her voice down as she threatened to take them back to the room without breakfast if they didn't stop playing with their food. It was chaotic, but somehow comforting, to focus on the mundane task of eating, and by unspoken consent we avoided talking about the case.

We adults had finished our food and, with the exception of Alma, who was still coaxing the twins to finish their home fried potatoes, were enjoying our second coffee, when Bennie Suarez walked to the table and bent over to speak to me.

"*Senor* Al," he said in a voice just above a whisper. "My cousin wishes to meet with you. He says it is very important."

"Where and when?" I asked.

"He said the same place as the last time. I am to call him to let him know when you can be there."

I looked at Buster. "Ten minutes?" He nodded. I looked up at Suarez. "Ten minutes."

"Very well," he said. "I will tell him."

"What's that all about?" Heather asked, as Suarez walked away.

"Your guess is as good as mine," I said. I stood.

Buster looked at Alma, who simply shrugged and smiled. She was a veteran cop's wife. She knew the drill. Quincy gave me a quizzical look. I shrugged. He went back to sipping his coffee.

"Call me if you need me," he said after putting his cup back on the table.

"Yeah," Heather said. "Let me know if you learn anything useful.

"Be careful," Alma said. She was looking at Buster, but I knew she included me in her warning.

Buster and I went out to the parking lot.

"We takin' your wheels?" he asked.

My bright green Volkswagen beetle isn't exactly inconspicuous, but it was unlikely to draw as much attention as Buster's, with the two toddler seats in the back. "Mine, of course," I said.

One thing about small towns that I like, probably the only thing, is that traffic is light. What the locals call a traffic jam is more than three cars at a traffic light at the same time. I pulled into the park eight minutes after leaving the spa. I didn't see a police car. I parked near the rear of the parking lot, and we got out and walked to the clearing behind the little copse of trees.

Five minutes later I heard the throaty roar of a souped-up engine, not the road racer type, the kind of engine that' s under the hood of a police cruiser. I looked around the trees, just as Williams brought his car to a stop. The front doors and one rear door opened. Williams got out of the driver's side, and his partner, Lewis, the passenger side. The doctor who'd examined the corpse at the restaurant, dressed now in a rumpled brown suit, got out of the rear seat on the driver's side.

Williams saw us first. He waved. "Hey, Mr. Pennyback, Detective Mayweather," he said. "Sorry for bothering you so early in the morning, but the Doc Johnson came up with something I figured you two would want to know right away."

"No problem," I said. "And, you can drop

the titles. I'm Al and he's Buster. We don't go in for a lot of ceremony. Now, what'd the doc come up with?"

Lewis and Johnson had come up to us then. "Better he tells you himself," Williams said. "Doc, you wanna tell Mr., er, Al and Buster, what you told me and Cory?"

Johnson took a folded document from his jacket pocket. He unfolded it and held it out toward me.

"This," he said. "Is my autopsy report on one Vivienne LeClerc."

"Shouldn't that go to the chief of police or the city attorney?" I asked.

"Don't worry, son, this is a copy. I might be old, but I'm not stupid. Now, do you want to know what's in it or not?"

I'd always thought the grouchy old country doctor was a myth made up to add human interest to TV shows, but here was one staring up into my face. The guy could have come from central casting. Okay, I thought, I'll see your grouchy country doctor, and raise you one hard-as-nails private eye.

"Of course I want to know what's in it," I said. "I figure it has to be interesting, or you wouldn't have dragged me all the way out here."

Johnson did a double take, and then the old codger smiled. "Okay, then, glad to know I'm working with a man who doesn't pull his punches." He switched the file to his left hand and stuck out his right. "Please to make your acquaintance, Mr. Pennyback."

I grasped his hand. It was warm and dry, and his grip was strong. "It's just plain Al, Dr. Johnson."

"Okay, Just Plain Al, I'm must Tobias, now what say we go over to that picnic table and take a load off, and I'll tell you about LeClerc's autopsy."

After we were seated, I held up a hand to stop Johnson who had spread the report on the table. "Before we get into that, I need to tell the three of you what we've discovered. First, the victim's name is not Vivienne LeClerc, and she's not French. She's Cora Lee Gables of Topeka, Kansas, and she's a grifter."

"Damn, now that really throws a wrinkle in . . . okay, let's put that aside a moment, and let me tell you what I found during autopsy. I'll skip the physical details, race, sex, body size, and crap like that. What matters is that the cause of death was, as you might expect, extreme hypothermia . . . in other words, she froze to death."

"Shoot, doc, we already know that," Buster said.'

Johnson gave him his crotchety look. "Buster, right? You're the impatient type, I can tell. Now, Al here, he's more to my liking. He waits patiently while an old man tells the story his way."

Buster ducked his head like he'd been smacked on the nose with a rolled up newspaper. Damn, someone besides Alma who could put him back in his cage. I was beginning to like Tobias Johnson.

"Go ahead and tell us your story, Tobias," I said.

"Okay, I was just about to get to the part you *don't* know," he said. "It's likely Vivienne, er, Cora Lee, never regained consciousness. In other words, she was out of it when her systems shut down from the extreme cold, and she passed peacefully. Now, that brings us to *why* she was unconscious. She was hit in the face, just in front of and above the temple, with a square-shaped, flat object, something heavy, and she was hit with enough force to cause extensive internal bleeding, oh, and unconsciousness."

"Doc, Tobias, could she have hit her head hard enough falling against one of those boxes in that freezer to knock her out like that?"

"Sure, she could have, but not hard enough to cause the bruising and damage I saw when I examined her skull." I looked at him, eyebrows raised. "I mean, young fellow, that the only way I can think she got a bruise like that is either she was shoved or swung against something, or someone swung a hard object and hit her head."

"Did you share this finding with the chief of police?"

"Of course I did, yesterday evening, I called him."

"And, his reaction?"

Johnson snorted. "Well, I'm here, so I figure you can guess what his reaction was. That stubborn, no strike that, that stupid son of a bitch is still treating this as an accident. This was no accident. That woman was murdered, pure and simple."

"Can't you convince the city attorney, or someone higher, to treat it as a homicide?"

"If I value my job, I can't go to the county or state folks, and Chief Holiday's got the city attorney in his pocket. Cory here told me what you and Buster were doing, when I bitched to him last night about the chief's non-reaction to my findings, so I'm bringing this to you. If this case is gonna be solved, it's for sure old lard butt's not gonna be the one to do it."

"You know you're putting your career at risk by this?"

"Son, I'm an old man. I got my private practice. I do this city coroner stuff on the side. It'd mean a cut in income, but I wouldn't starve. It's these two youngsters who're really in jeopardy."

"Now, doc, I already told you, we're doing what's right, so quite worrying," Williams said. Lewis's head bobbed up and down.

"See what I mean, Al, if these youngsters can risk it, how do you expect me to sit by and do nothing?"

"Welcome to the team, doc."

TWENTY-THREE

Heather came rushing breathlessly from the elevator as Buster and I entered the spa lobby.

"Oh, am I glad to see you two," she said, rushing up to us. "I tried calling you on your mobiles, but kept getting an 'out of service area' signal."

"Slow down, Heather," I said. "What's the problem?"

Her smile was so wide it stretched the skin under her eyes. "Not a problem, far from it. I identified the person who sent that strange email to Cora Lee Gables, and it is a local."

"That's great, kiddo. Who is it?"

She pursed her lips and put her hands on her hips. "Aw, come on, can't I at least tell

you how I did it first? It was brilliant
detective work."

It's not that we had anywhere to be, so it
was only fair that she got the chance to
showcase her skills.

"Okay, Miss Sherlock Holmes, take us
through your amazing feat."

"No need to be sarcastic," she said. "And,
it's *Ms.* Sherlock Holmes if you don't mind.
Now, here's how I did it." We walked as she
talked, and finally settled in the spot that
had sort of become ours, the little nook
behind the spreading ferns in the large vases.
"I decided to take a break from poring
through the stuff on Cora's computer, and do
some more background checks. I was doing a
check on that guy, Gavin Laine, when I had
one of those 'eureka' moments. You'll never
guess what Laine's full name is." She waited,
but neither Buster nor I spoke. "Aw, come on
guys, guess his full name."

She was obviously having fun, and
milking this for all she could, so I decided to
play along. That's how at loose ends I was.
"Gavin Murgatroyd Laine?"

"No."

"Gavin Abraham Lincoln Laine," said
Buster, joining in on the fun.

"No, silly, not even close."

"Well, I give up," I said. I raised my hands
in surrender. "So, tell me, what is Gavin
Laine's full name."

"It's Gavin Edward Laine. I found it when I

pulled up his driver's license records."

"So, you found his full name, so what does—, holy shit, GEL69 is Gavin Edward Laine. Laine's the one who sent that email to our victim."

"Bingo!" she said.

"Son of a bitch," Buster said. "That's the guy that didn't want Bob opening his restaurant."

"One and the same," I said. "And, since getting rid of the head chef might be seen as a way to interfere with the opening, even if it didn't stop it that gives him a motive."

Buster's facial expression was stormy. He slammed his left fist into his right palm. "Maybe we oughta pay him a visit," he said.

"Whoa, pardner, let's chill our jets a minute. All we have right now is supposition. Now, we all think this guy's as good a suspect as Muncie, better in fact, but before we go off half-cocked, we need to know more."

He looked at me under dangerously lowered brows. "Yeah, and a visit to him, for a little chat, might just tell us what we need to know."

Now, I know for a fact that Buster doesn't use physical force on suspects. But, he's not above threatening it if he thinks it might make them talk. In Laine's case, I didn't know the man well enough to know if that would work, and it's not my first preference. Any kind of intimidation when you're trying to get information out of people is risky. You can never trust the information you get, and the problem with threatening force is that you have to be willing to carry out that threat in case a suspect calls your bluff. Get caught bluffing and your credibility is in the crapper.

"I think maybe it'd be best if I went to see him alone," I said. "That way, he wouldn't feel pressured, and I might catch him off guard."

He pouted, but gave in. Not, though, without one last parting shot. "If your way don't work, we doin' it my way."

Rizzoli's was a squat, rectangular building of dark brown vertical wood shingles. Its parking lot was cordoned off from the rest of the complex by chains attached to metal poles set in cement bases, with little signs attached informing one and all that the parking within was for Rizzoli's customers only, and all others would be towed. Laine certainly seemed to like exclusivity. Not that it was doing him any good; there were only ten cars in his 'exclusive' parking lot, and in a building the size of his, even if each car contained four people, his place would look empty.

And empty is what it looked. The dining space, some forty feet across and twenty feet from front entrance to the marble and mahogany bar in the back, had at least thirty circular tables, each with four chairs, and only five tables had customers. With the two guys in ill-fitting suits hunched over drinks at the bar, the customers were still outnumbered by the staff, ten bored looking waitresses, four busboys standing around with nothing to do, and two bartenders, one of whom stood near the cash register with a glazed look that made me think he was probably asleep on his feet. Fantastic Fusions had just opened, so it was unlikely it had impacted Laine's business that quickly. No, it looked to me like the locals just weren't all that into Italian food, and a big menu board at the entrance listing the specials showed that Italian food was all Rizzoli's offered.

As I stepped in, a hawk-faced man with slicked back hair and a slight paunch hanging over his black trousers, stepped out of the shadows. "Good morning, sir," he said. "Do you have a reservation?"

I looked around the room and all the empty tables. Poor guy must've been given instructions to ask everyone that, and he hadn't yet realized how stupid it sounded.

"No, I'm not here to eat," I said. "I need to speak with the owner, Gavin Laine."

His mouth dropped open and he blinked like I'd just blown dust into his eyes.

"Is he in?" I asked.

"Uh, he's in his office, I think. You got an appointment?"

"No, but I have important information for him that I'm sure he'll want to hear."

He looked hesitant, but I stood my

ground, staring levelly into his beady eyes. Finally, he called the nearest bored-looking, gum-chewing waitress over.

"Betty, go tell Mr. Laine there's some guy here says he's got an important message."

Without breaking the tempo of her jaw movements, she pushed herself off the wall and went, hips swaying under the short black mini-skirt, toward a door to the right of the bar. A few seconds later, she returned, still chewing and stopped in front of hawk-face so suddenly her breasts underneath the frilly-collared white blouse threatened to bounce out.

"Boss said tell him to come on back," she said.

Hawk-face looked disappointed. Minions are like that. They like to flaunt their power, and it really pisses them off when they discover that they have none.

"Okay," he said. "Show him the way, Betty."

Based on her expression, usher wasn't in her job description, but before she could say anything, hawk-face had melted back into the shadowy recess next to the door and was studiously ignoring me. She shrugged, causing her breasts to bounce again.

"Follow me," she said.

I did, and it wasn't an unpleasant experience. Our parade across the floor went unnoticed by the diners at the tables, but I noticed that both of the men at the bar tracked my movement. They weren't even trying to be discrete about it either. As I passed the bar, I noticed a bulge in the rumpled jacket of the nearest. He was carrying, and a fairly large caliber weapon from the size of the bulge. He made no move toward it, though, so I ignored him, while still watching him with my peripheral vision, until I'd passed through the door behind Betty's still swaying hips. She led me past two closed doors and stopped before an unadorned door in the middle of the hallway on the left wall. She rapped on the door.

"Come in," a muffled voice on the other side of the door said.

"Go on in," she said, and she brushed past me as she left, confirming what I'd suspected when she jiggled the first time, she wasn't wearing a bra. She smiled when I flinched, and put a little extra sway on as she walked away.

I tore my eyes away from the pendulum-like movements and pushed the door open.

The door to his office was plain, but Laine's office was anything but plain. The distance from the door to his huge, mahogany desk was a good fifteen feet. On top of it was a space-age looking phone console with five rows of buttons and a large speaker grille, next to a sleek laptop computer. To his right was a large wet bar with two rows of expensive liquor bottles, a silver ice bucket and a tray with eight crystal glasses. Below the bar was a small refrigerator. To the left of the desk was a wooden console, above which were mounted six video monitors showing various parts of the restaurant. Laine sat in a large, black leather executive chair, his attention focused on the leftmost monitor that showed the bar and the two rumpled guys sitting on stools near the end. From the angle of their heads it appeared they were looking at the door through which I'd just come and their expressions were anything but friendly.

I crossed the room, making swishing sounds on the thick plush carpet.

Without taking his attention from the monitor, Laine waved me toward a chair on the right side of his desk.

"Have a seat," he said. "You're one of Campbell's friends, right?"

"Well, more like a friend of a friend of his," I said. "My name's Al Pennyback. My friend, Campbell's friend, is DC Police Detective Buster Mayweather."

I watched his face as I spoke. His brow twitched microscopically as I mentioned Buster.

"I see. So, Mr. Pennyback, what can I do for you?"

His attention was still on the monitors, specifically the monitor showing the two men at the bar, and he looked . . . worried or frightened.

"Mr. Campbell's concerned about his

liability insurance, so he asked Buster and me to do our own investigation of Vivienne LeClerc's death."

"Yeah, I can understand that. Her next of kin's liable to sue the pants off the restaurant, not to mention OSHA reaming little Bobby for an employee freezing to death in his place.

For a fraction of a second there was a look of pleasure in his eyes, but it was quickly replaced by worry.

"So, why do you want to talk to me?"

"We're talking to everyone who knew . . . Vivienne LeClerc."

For the first time, he pulled his attention away from the monitors. He swiveled his chair and stared intently at me.

"I maybe met the broad, what, two times," he said. "I didn't really *know* her. There's nothing I can tell you."

His eyes darted right and up as he spoke, just a fraction of a second's movement, but enough for me to know that he was lying.

"Maybe you knew her as Cora Lee Gables," I said.

His eyebrows twitched; again, just a little, but it hit home. He recognized the name.

"Who is that?" he asked. "I don't know anyone by that name."

"Really, that's interesting, considering you sent her two emails."

Up to that point, his expressions had been micro-expressions, measured in milliseconds, but now his mouth dropped open, and he stared at me.

"What? You're surprised that we know about your correspondence with her? What did you two talk about at your little meeting?"

He let out a long breath.

"You don't know what you're messing with, Mr. Pennyback," he said. "If you know what's good for you, you'll leave this alone and go back where you came from."

"Funny, your chief of police keeps telling me the same thing."

"Hah, that fat fuck's nothing but hot air. I'm talking about a real hornet's nest that you really don't wanna be sticking your hands into."

"Would you care to be a little more specific?"

Fear flickered across his face.

"No, but if you're smart, you'll get in your car and go back home."

"Well, I have this little problem," I said. "Once I start working on a problem, I don't stop until I've solved it. Right now, a part of my problem is how you tumbled onto the fact that Vivienne LeClerc was in fact Cora Lee Gables, and what was it you said to her at that meeting you demanded."

"I got nothing to say to you, Pennyback. Now, you get the hell out of my restaurant before I have you thrown out."

I smiled and leaned forward.

"You wouldn't be referring to the two bozos sitting at the bar, would you? Unless you've got a good employee health insurance policy, I wouldn't advise it. They don't look like they could handle themselves against a troop of cub scouts."

"You don't know what you're messing with. This is bigger than the both of us," he said. "Now, would you please get out of here?"

I'd half expected him to call the two goons to throw me out. Had he been bluffing, and when I called it, backed down.

Something had him spooked to the point of almost pissing his pants, and it had to do with Cora Lee Gables. I knew it like I know my own name, I just couldn't prove it—yet.

Charles Ray

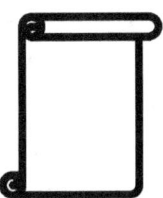

TWENTY-FOUR

I left Laine sitting there staring at the monitor. The two goons at the bar gave me the evil eye as I walked past them on my way out, but did nothing to hamper my passage. They watched me, though. I could feel their scrutiny like hot pokers drilling into my back until the door closed behind me and I was in the parking lot. I would have bet that they'd gone to a window and watched me as I crossed the parking lot and made my way back to the spa.

Buster and Heather were still sitting in the alcove. She had a cup of tea, and Buster was holding a glass of yellow liquid up and looking at the large chandelier through it.

"Whatcha get out of Laine?" he asked as I lowered myself into the chair across from him.

"He's the one who sent the emails all right, but I couldn't get him to divulge details."

"Told you I shoulda gone with you. I'd have made that mother sing like an Italian tenor."

"That might've been a bit difficult," I said. "He had muscle in the restaurant, two mean looking goons, and they were both packing."

He put his lemonade down and looked at me, his brown brow furrowed. "You shittin' me? Why a guy own a restaurant need armed guards?"

"I've been asking myself that question, but I can't come up with an answer that makes sense."

"Still, you shoulda took me with you," he said. "I coulda took care of them shitheads."

"You know, Buster Mayweather," Heather said. "Your language is getting terrible, and I don't just mean your grammar. Do you kiss Alma with that potty mouth of yours?"

"Shoot, Heather, you've heard worse."

He tried to act like her words hadn't stung, but the look in his eyes said they had. I know that his lapse into a sort of street patois is just his way of relaxing with people he thinks of as friends, and his profanity is a way to let off steam, something he can't do with his kids around. I wasn't sure Heather did until I noticed her start to smile.

"You men are so freakin' easy," she said. "Like putty in our hands."

Buster's face broke into a grin. "Heather Bunche, I'm gonna get you for that, you just wait and see."

"Before you start plotting your revenge, maybe you ought to sit back and listen. I think I know why Laine has armed guards, and I don't think you're gonna like it too much."

Buster cocked his head to the side and grinned wolfishly. "What, you gonna tell us these dudes are mafia or something?"

Heather's head snapped around and she glared at him. "Have you been sneaking in and looking at my notes, because if you have, that's just . . . dirty pool, Buster."

It took a second for her words to sink in.

"Heather," I said. "Are you saying that these guys *are* mob?"

"I can't say with a hundred percent certainty." She shrugged. "But, I ran across information when I was researching Laine that I didn't pay much attention to, but when you mentioned guys with guns, I remembered it."

"Tell us about it," Buster said.

"I'm not speaking to you."

"Hey, I didn't snoop through your things," he said. "I was just being a smart mouth, you know. That just popped out."

"You swear you haven't looking through my stuff?"

"Cross my heart and hope to die, now tell us why you think Laine's connected."

She looked at him as if she didn't believe his apology, then she smiled that languid Cheshire cat smile again.

"Well, his background is not all that different from any other middle class resident of Lakeview. He grew up here, and after high school, went off to New York City where he got a bachelor's degree in business at CUNY. He worked as a bank teller and then a restaurant manager in Little Italy for a while before coming back home." She reached for her ever-present notepad and opened it to a page near the middle. "He married his high school girlfriend when he came back to Lakeview, but they got divorced three years later, and that was about the time things got strange."

"Strange, how?" I asked.

"Well, he managed a little roadside café north of town, but right after his wife left him, he bought Rizzoli's, and has moved up in the world since. I mean, he wasn't exactly trailer trash, but he was hardly what you'd call well off. He and his wife lived in a small house not far from the café he managed. After she left him, he bought a big house in one of the more exclusive parts of town."

Buster was shaking his head.

"Man must've had a damn good lawyer to get divorced and still have enough bread to buy a new house."

That I couldn't disagree with, and without knowing more, it just left a lot of questions.

"You make a good point, Buster." I pointed a finger at Heather, making sure to smile as I did so. "Heather, see if you can dig up information on Laine's divorce, and while you're at it, get an address of the ex-wife."

"I can probably get an address in a few minutes. You guys want to wait here, or go to my room so I can access my computer?"

In the interest of saving time, we decided to follow her to her room. Once inside, she wasted no time getting her computer fired up. After cycling through a few screens; far too fast for me to read; she sat back with a smile on her face. "Voila, I have it. Rebecca Stone, formerly Mrs. Rebecca Laine, lives in Mayville, just a few miles northwest of here." She wrote an address on a blank page in her notepad, tore it out and handed it to me. "I have her phone number if you want to call her first."

"No, I think I'll just drop in on her. That way, she won't have time to wonder why we want to talk to her."

"You know, it might be a good idea for me to go along with you," she said. "She might be more willing to talk about her failed marriage to another woman."

As much as I would've rather she stay at her computer looking up information, she made a valid point. Neither Buster nor I had much experience in that arena.

"Okay, you can come along, but as soon as we get back here, I want you to get to digging into Laine's financials. I have a feeling that it's somehow related to the murder of Cora Gables."

TWENTY-FIVE

We piled into my Volkswagen. Buster and Heather argued over who would ride shotgun, but his longer legs won out, and Heather grudgingly sat in the back.

The land between Lakeview and Mayville was mostly wooded or farms, with a few houses on the shore of Chautauqua Lake on our left. Traffic was light, mostly pickup trucks and older model cars, until we entered the outskirts of Mayville, where it picked up, with later model cars, vans, and commercial trucks.

Heather had used a computer program to get directions to Rebecca Stone's place, off a side street heading north at the east end of

Mayville. We turned between a gas station and a convenience store that dominated the corner, and entered a fading working class neighborhood of older one- and two-story wood frame houses with postage stamp-sized lawns and fenced backyards. The street was lined with gnarled hardwood trees whose limbs hung down perilously close to the sidewalk, forcing pedestrians to either duck or move to the street to pass in places.

Stone's house was a white one-story house with blue shutters and green roof, with several panels missing, and an attached one-car garage. The yard looked like it hadn't been mowed in a week or more, and there was a green plastic trash container blocking the driveway. Buster jumped out and moved the container against the garage door, and I pulled up close and cut the engine.

Heather and I got out and joined Buster. The three of us walked to the front door. The wooden door was scuffed at the bottom and the red paint was flaking, with large chips hanging loose. The same was true of the outside walls. In several places, the white paint had chipped away, revealing grayed and weathered wood. If Rebecca Stone got a generous divorce settlement, she certainly hadn't used it on housing.

I stepped up and rang the doorbell.

After a few seconds, I heard the scuffling sound of footsteps on a hard surface, and then the door swung inward.

The woman who stood in the doorway was as short as Heather, about five-three, but outweighed her by a good hundred pounds. Her thighs bulged against the brown ankle-length slacks she wore, her belly pushed against the off-white shirt worn outside the slacks, her feet bulged over a worn pair of pink slippers, and she had enough chins to supply a rifle squad and have two or three left over. Her bloodshot eyes were almost hidden in her bulging pink cheeks. She held a half-empty shot glass in her pudgy hands. Her nails were ragged and the last polish she'd applied at some point in the distant past was cracked.

"Yeah, what can I do for you folks?" she asked. She had a whiskey voice, not the sexy kind, the ragged, rough around the edges kind of voice that sounded like a dying frog at the bottom of a well, and when she spoke, the stale liquor smell from her mouth made my eyes water.

"Are you Rebecca Stone?" I asked.

"Yeah, who wants to know?"

"Ma'am, we'd like to ask you a few questions about your former husband, Gavin Laine, if you don't mind," I said.

She lifted the glass, draining it and then glared up at me. "Why you want to ask me about that slime bag? Who the fuck are you, anyway?"

She looked like she wanted to hit me in the face with the empty glass. Before she could, though, Heather stepped forward and stood between us.

"Ma'am, we're sorry to drop in unannounced like this, but my associates and I are investigating a . . . suspicious death in Lakeview, and we think your ex-husband might be involved," she said.

"What are you, some kind of cop?"

Heather pulled her PI card from her jacket pocket and held it up, using her finger to cover the Maryland=District of Columbia-Virginia caveat, but clearly showing her photo and the title, 'Private Investigator.' "I'm a private investigator, ma'am, as is my associate, Al Pennyback. The silent gentleman behind us is Detective Lieutenant Buster Mayweather. He's a homicide investigator."

I was impressed. She was being truthful, just leaving out the fact that none of us had jurisdiction in New York. She sounded so official I felt like standing to attention. It also had an impact on Rebecca Stone. She relaxed and looked at Heather with eye-gaping, slack-jawed admiration.

"A girl private eye? Now, ain't that something." She stepped aside. "Why don't you come on in and have a seat?"

She stepped aside and allowed us to enter. Her living room was a study in clutter. Clothing, old newspapers, and empty whiskey bottles were all over the place, and it smelled like a dive bar at closing time.

She felt around under the sofa and found a bottle that was still half full. Waving at the two ratty chairs, she plopped herself down on one end of the couch, making a 'whoosh' sound as her fat ass sank into the cushion, and unscrewed to top.

"Have a seat." She waved the bottle at Heather. The smell from her underarms made her breath almost smell good. "You sit here on the couch with me, honey. You folks want a drink?" We all shook our heads no. "S'fine; means more for me." She took a long pull from the bottle.

I pushed a dirty bra off one chair, and Buster carefully brushed at the seat of the other. Heather looked tentatively at the other end of the sofa, and finally eased herself down. The cushions made a sighing sound as she sat.

"Okay, now whaddya wanna know 'bout that no-good rat of an ex-husband of mine?"

Wiggling a bit to adjust her behind on what looked like a slightly greasy cushion Heather made a face and leaned forward. "Well, Ms. Stone, as I said, we're investigating a suspicious death in Lakeview. Your ex-husband had a . . . relationship with the victim, so we—"

"Was the victim a broad?" Stone asked.

"Well, yes, as a matter of fact. How did you know that?"

"It just figures. Gavin always had a wandering eye, but he has absolutely no respect for women. Find 'em, fuck 'em, and forget 'em, that's his motto. Look what that shit heel did to me. Kicked me outta the house, divorced me, and didn't give me shit. I'll bet the dead broad refused to get out when he asked her to, and he killed her."

"Well, we're not sure." Heather held a hand up to stop the torrent of words pouring from the woman. "Ms. Stone, what was the reason for your divorce from your husband?"

Stone took another long swallow from the bottle. She burped and wiped her mouth with the back of her hand.

"*He* said irreconcilable differences, whatever the fuck that is. He paid the judge off, and that old fart agreed with everything he said."

Heather reached over to pat her arm, looked down at the dirty streaks, and withdrew her hand. "What kind of settlement did you get out of it?"

After making a 'snuff' sound, Stone wiped at her eyes and leaned her head back against the sofa cushion. "Settlement . . . settlement?" Her head dipped from side to side and she closed her eyes. I thought she was going to pass out, but Heather just overcame her aversion to the grime on the woman's arm to lay her hand on it and remain silent. Finally she opened her eyes. They glistened with tears hovering on the brink of cascading down her florid cheeks. "That bastard gave me fifty thousand dollars and let me take my clothes and jewelry, and he had me sign an agreement that I would never contact him again. Can you believe that shit? Fifty grand's hardly enough to stay afloat, and I got no skills." She sniffed loudly. "I have to stay in this shit hole 'cause I can't afford to rent or buy a decent place. Settlement? That bastard was suddenly rolling in dough, and he kicked me to the curb. When we first got married, and he was struggling to make ends meet with that diner, it was okay having me around. Then he met those guinea bastards and I was no longer good enough for him."

She began sobbing quietly, tears flowing freely across her cheeks, leaving little trails in the grime. At that point, I was glad Heather had insisted on coming along. Not only had she known how to get the woman to open up, but I was at a loss with a crying woman. Heather, though, just sat there, patting her hand and making little 'tsk, tsk' sounds.

"The way he treated you was, is, terrible," Heather said. "Who were these . . . guineas he met?"

"I don't know for sure, just some Eye-talians from New York." More sniffing; and she had to wipe away trails of slime leaking from both flared nostrils. "Four of them showed up at our house one day. One sleazy looking little guy with slicked down hair and an expensive suit, and three goons that looked like they were uncomfortable in suits;

Gavin took 'em to the backyard where I couldn't hear what they were talkin' about. A week later, he's suddenly flashing more cash than I'd ever seen him in the same room with, and talkin' about buying that Eye-talian restaurant over near the lake. A month later, just after he opened the restaurant, he presented me with divorce papers. Said our marriage had run its course, and I wouldn't fit into his new life style." Her shoulders shook as she cried. "Have you ever heard shit like that before? I gave that son of a bitch the best years of my life. Stood by him when we didn't hardly have a pot to piss in, then when he hits it rich, he dumps me."

She leaned forward and put her head between her knees and began sobbing loudly. Heather rubbed her back.

"There, there, Rebecca," she said. "It's terrible what he did to you, but men can be such pigs." She glanced quickly at Buster and me; a warning not to react to her words, and a little half smile to let us know that she wasn't referring to us. "Tell me, these Italians from New York; other than being bad dressers, what else can you tell me about them?"

God, this girl was good! She kept her voice low and sympathetic, spoke soothing words that seemed to calm Stone a bit, but kept on target to get the information we sought.

Stone raised her head and looked at Heather. I can only describe her expression as a cry for help. "Them, hell if you'd seen 'em, you'd know. And, I'm not being prejudiced against Eye-talians when I say this, 'cause I know not all of them are involved, but these guys were mob. That stupid prick, Gavin, has gone and gotten himself in bed with the Eye-talian Mafia."

Heather looked confused. "Why would the mafia be interested in a small town restaurant owner?"

She's a whiz on the computer, has a network that rivals the CIA, and an IQ that's probably off the charts, but if it's not something she's had reason to research, Heather's a babe in the woods. I, though, not nearly as smart, picked up bits and pieces of sometimes useless junk in my perambulations on the streets of the city, junk that on occasion turns out to be valuable. *I* knew why the mob would be interested in a restaurant, or any other business, in a small town, especially a small town in close proximity to the Canadian border. City officials in small towns, most of them receiving meager salaries, would be relatively easy to corrupt or intimidate, and being close to the border would make it easy for the mob to move whatever they needed to move, drugs, guns, money, or people.

"Did you ever find out what the people from New York wanted from your husband?" I asked.

She shook her head. "No. I asked him

once, and he near to bit my head off. Told me to mind my business. That was the week before he served me with divorce papers."

There was nothing more useful we could get from her, but it was pointing us in a useful direction. If Gavin Laine was involved with the mob, and he had something dirty on Gables, it was possible, just possible, that he had a reason to kill her. But, for some reason, it just didn't seem to fit.

I stood, wincing at the tacky feeling on the back of my trouser legs. "Thank you for your time, Ms. Stone," I said. "Sorry again for dropping in unannounced."

"No problem," she said. She didn't move from the couch as Buster and Heather also stood. "Just do me one favor."

"If I can. What's the favor?"

"If you can prove that that skunk did kill someone, and you get to him before the cops do, could you maybe bust him up a little, and give him my best regards when you do?"

She wasn't joking. I didn't answer her, merely nodded in a noncommittal way, and let her make of it what she willed. She had her head back and the bottle at her lips as we walked out. At the rate she was chugging liquor down, she would probably have forgotten our visit before we were out of the neighborhood.

Buster was shaking his head as we walked back to the car.

"I sorta feel sorry for her," he said. "But,

I'm not sure I blame Laine for dumping her."

Heather punched his arm. "Come on, she's been through a lot. She's probably like that because of the way Laine treated her."

He shook his head. "You got a lot to learn, little sis. Ain't no way she put on all that flab since the divorce, and the way she's drinking; she didn't learn that overnight."

She screwed up her eyes and looked at me. I just shrugged. Heather's a committed feminist, and there was no way I was joining that argument. The sad thing is, I agreed with Buster. Getting dumped probably tipped her over the edge, but from the looks of her, she was already teetering before the fall.

Charles Ray

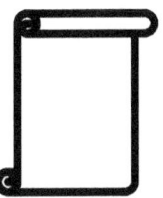

TWENTY-SIX

An hour later we were back in Heather's room. She was at the desk hunched over her laptop, Buster sat on the chair near the sliding door leading out onto the balcony, and I was sitting on the foot of the bed.

"Looks like this dude Laine's good for killing Cora," Buster said.

"I don't know, bro," I said. "There's something about this that's bugging me."

"What? You sayin' you don't think Laine did it? Man, he's connected. Maybe she found out, and he got rid of her to keep her from talkin'."

"That's what I'm saying, I'm afraid." He looked shocked. "Listen to me a minute. It's pretty clear he's got mob connections, probably running drugs or laundering money through his restaurant. But, I don't see how Gables could have found that out if the local cops don't know." His face got tense. That was a sign that he was thinking about what I'd just said. "In addition, Gables' death doesn't have the hallmarks of a mob hit. If the mob wants you gone, they either do it bloody and public, or you disappear."

His eyes went wide. He was getting it. "Yeah, I see what you mean. Somebody knocked her out and either left her in the freezer or put her there. No way they could be sure somebody wouldn't find her before she died."

"Wow!" Heather said. "Wow!"

"What?" Buster and I asked in unison.

She looked uneasy. "I, uh, just happened to get into Samuel Holiday's email account, and I saw something disturbing."

"I don't want to know *how* you did that, do I?"

"Yeah . . . probably not, that way, if I get caught, you can say you knew nothing about it. Anyway, don't you want to know what I found?"

I nodded. "Sure, tell me what you found about our esteemed chief of police."

"Well, I was just looking through his accounts. He deletes his incoming and outgoing emails regularly, but like most people, he neglects to then delete them from his Trash folder. Most email accounts clean that folder out automatically every thirty days. I didn't see anything in his in or outbox, so just for kicks I took a look at Trash, and there's where I found an interesting string of correspondence over the past three weeks."

Buster scooted his chair closer and cocked his head.

"Lemme guess," he said. "That string shows he's a dirty cop?"

"Big time. He's been in correspondence with a Russian in Yonkers, and while the guy doesn't put Russian Mob in his signature block, it's pretty clear that he is part of the mob. The email talks about establishing competition with the Italians here in Lakeview, and orders Holiday to take care of their agent who is here to facilitate it."

"Do they give the name of the agent?" I asked. "If we can identify him we have something we can take to the feds. They love investigating crooked local officials."

"No, it doesn't, and it's not a 'him.' They want Holiday to look out for 'her.'

"Shit," Buster said, jumping to his feet. "A woman; competition against the Italians. Bro, you know what that means?"

I sure as hell did. Suddenly, several things became crystal clear. "Carol Lee Gables was here on behalf of the Russian mob. They were planning on setting your friend's restaurant up as a franchise."

"Well, that explains why a grifter would be targeting a restaurant," Heather said. "It still doesn't tell us who killed her."

Buster snapped his fingers. "Maybe they found out she met with Laine and thought she was rattin' on 'em, so they took her out."

"No, I don't think so. If anything, the Russian mob's worse than the mafia when it comes to dealing with traitors. If they'd done it, it would have been pretty bloody. No, we got several things going here; the Italian mafia with a base here and the Russians trying to muscle in. Now, that could get messy. But, I don't think Gables' death has anything to do with that."

"Shit, they puts us back to square one," he said, plopping down. He had a dejected look on his face, which probably mirrored my own. "What the hell we gonna do now?"

What I felt like doing was breaking heads. It was frustrating to have so many suspects suddenly evaporate, and have a case fall apart before my very eyes. We'd run around in a big circle, only to find ourselves right back where we started.

"What if it was personal?" Heather asked.

"Huh?' Buster said.

"Explain," I said.

"Well, at the start, you thought maybe it was Walter Muncie. As far as I'm concerned he's still number-one suspect," she said. "But, we should also take another look at the other employees of the restaurant, all of whom have access to that freezer."

Of course. I should have thought of that. But then, that's why Heather and I are a team. What I miss, she catches, and sometimes, vice versa. And, it made sense. We'd gotten so fixated on the organized crime connection that I'd neglected to look closely at the crime. Gables had been hit hard enough to cause bleeding in her skull, and then left unconscious in the freezer. Maybe there'd been no intent to kill her. Or maybe it was what my brain was now telling me it was; a crime of passion. Jealousy is a passion, a passion that can lead to hate and murder. That alone put Muncie back in the number one spot.

"Okay, we need to go back and talk to each of them, starting with Muncie. But, before we do, there are a couple of loose ends I'd like to tie up."

Charles Ray

TWENTY-SEVEN

I had Heather go to the spa business center and print copies of the emails from Holiday's account and the emails Laine had sent to Cora Gables. I then had Suarez call his cousin and arrange a meeting, but instead of meeting at the park outside town, I asked for Williams and Lewis to come to the reception area of the spa. If things worked out like I planned, we would no longer have to meet in secret.

Quincy had gone around the lake to visit Chautauqua Institute, a place that had been built in the 1800s by a bunch of rich business people and clerics from the Methodist Church as a place where their families could spend the summers enriching their minds and souls. The Institute started the first public book clubs in America and over the years had been converted to a general cultural institution with programs ranging from politics to religion, mostly in the summers. In law school, Quincy had dated a girl whose family owned a house there, and he'd been invited to stay with them one summer. He said he hadn't seen the place in over fifteen years and wanted to see how it had changed. So, that just left Heather, Buster and me to meet the two Lakeview cops. We went down to our little nook. We ordered coffee and waited.

Williams and Lewis showed up thirty minutes later. They looked around nervously as they entered the lobby. I stood to get their attention, and waved them over.

"Are you sure meeting in public like this is a good idea?" Williams said. "If word gets back to Chief Holiday that we were here, it could mean our badges."

They were clearly nervous, but just the fact that they'd come in answer to my request anyway raised my opinion of them.

"Have a seat, fellows," I said. I waved the waiter over. "Would you like a cup of coffee?"

"No," Lewis said. "I don't think we should stay long."

They sat and turned their chairs so they could see the entrance.

"Gentlemen, I have some information to share with you that I think will obviate any threat your chief might make. In fact, when you see what we've dug up, I think you'll agree that change is coming to the Lakeview Police Department."

That got their attention pulled away from the entrance and to me. I laid out what we'd discovered, and showed them copies of Holiday's emails. As they read, their eyes were as round as saucers.

"Holy shit," Lewis said. "I always thought the chief was incompetent." He looked over his shoulder quickly. "But, this is . . . holy shit."

"What do you suggest we do about this, Al?" Williams asked.

"We need to arrest him," Williams said.

I held up a hand. "Agreed, but let's not be too hasty. The information we have now is circumstantial at best. We need to get the chief to implicate himself."

"How do you suggest we go about doing that?" Williams' young face was twisted with fury.

"I have an idea," I said. "Here's what we'll do."

Charles Ray

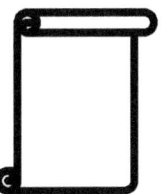

TWENTY-EIGHT

My plan was simple. I would approach Holiday alone, with Buster and the two young cops backing me up, and get him to make an incriminating statement. They could then swoop in and arrest him. That was the plan. Of course, I had no idea how I was going to get the man to confess—I'd just have to wing it, something, fortunately, I'm pretty good at.

Williams and Lewis informed me that Holiday wasn't at police headquarters. He'd called in and said he was taking a sick day, leaving the department under the control of the senior sergeant.

Before we left the spa, Williams suggested that I approach Holiday wearing a wire. He and his partner would be monitoring and recording the encounter from their car which would be parked nearby. This, he maintained, would not only enable them to respond quickly if need be, but would provide recorded evidence against their corrupt chief. Quincy wasn't there to consult with regarding the admissibility of evidence recorded like this without a warrant, but I liked the part about being able to respond in a hurry.

We left the spa in a convoy, with me leading and Buster riding in the police car following me. Following the directions Williams had given me, I left the parking lot, turned right into the town proper, and left on Main Street past neat shops and Mom and Pop stores out of town and into a whole different universe.

The wealthy citizens of Lakeview lived in an area called Willow Grove, an expansive area dotted with palatial houses, ranch, colonial, and modern styles on expansive, tree-covered lawns, many of them enclosed by brick walls too high to peer over. Even though there was no sign, you could tell when you entered Willow Grove. The grass was neater, the trees were trimmed precisely; even the streets and sidewalks were cleaner and brighter than the rest of the town.

A block from the two-story colonial structure that was Holiday's residence, the police car pulled over. Williams blinked his lights once. I drove on.

Holiday's house wasn't one with a wall, but it sat well back from the street with a winding driveway lined with privet hedges leading to the three-car attached garage. The walkway off the driveway, leading to the front porch, circled upon itself, and a stone fountain in the shape of an angel holding a bowl sat in the center of the circle.

I stopped, cut the engine and got out. The only sounds were the ticking of my cooling engine and the warbling of birds in the stately trees, a mixture of broadleaf and evergreens, surrounding the house. The lawn was lush green and immaculately maintained. Holiday had not only been able to afford the place, but from the looks of the grounds, could afford to pay someone to come in and keep it up. I couldn't see the fat cop mowing this expanse of grass himself.

When I thumbed the doorbell button I could hear chimes somewhere deep within the house playing some classic song. The door swung inwards. A short woman with stumpy legs, gray hair pulled back in a bun, wearing a blue dress and a white apron stood there looking at me like I was what the dog left behind and she'd just stepped in it.

"Can I help you?" She didn't sound like she wanted to help me.

"I'd like to speak with Chief Holiday," I said. "Is he at home?"

She gave me more of that 'why can't I scrub this shit off my shoe' look and made a sniffling sound before answering, "Yes he's here. If you'll wait I'll see if he wants to talk to you. What's your name?" I told her. Then, she closed the door in my face.

Shortly she was back, still looking at me with a sour expression, but she at least opened the door and stepped aside.

"Mr. Holiday said he'll talk to you on the patio. I'll show you the way."

I followed her through the house. As we passed through the large living room, I got a glimpse of a short, chubby blonde stuffed into a pair of blue shorts and almost falling out of a white blouse, going up the stairs.

Holiday was standing at the edge of a brown and white flagstone patio, a glass of amber liquid in his left hand, a large cigar in his right. Behind him, near the center of the patio, were a fold-out green and yellow plastic lounge and a red and white ice chest. A bottle of Kentucky Pride whiskey sat on top of the chest. He might have moved out of his working class neighborhood, but lots of it was still inside him. He didn't look especially pleased to see me.

"What do you want, Pennyback?"

He took a puff from the cigar, blowing the smoke in my direction, and then took a long drink from the glass.

"I'd like to talk to you about Vivienne LeClerc," I said. "Or, maybe you know her better as Cora Lee Gables."

He took it well, but, his hand shook just enough to slosh the liquid, and his left eyebrow twitched.

"You telling me that LeClerc wasn't her real name?"

His tone wavered just enough to convince me he was still lying through his teeth.

"I'm not telling you anything you don't already know, Holiday."

"How'm I supposed to know this . . . what did you call her, Coral Gables?"

"I'll give you credit for one thing, Holiday," I said. "You're a better liar than you are a police chief, but not by much. You're never gonna be able to explain to your Russian bosses how you let their asset get killed."

For a full second his face collapsed. He went pale, and this time, when his hand shook, the ice cubes in the glass clinked against the sides. He jammed the cigar into his mouth and took a long pull, and then blew the smoke out in a billowing gray cloud.

"You d-don't know what you're t-talkin' about," he said.

"Don't I? Didn't they tell you to look out for her? Some job you did. She's dead, and now the Russian's are gonna have to find someone else to run their operations out of Fantastic Fusions."

His eyes flickered from side to side. I had him in a corner, and he knew it. Like a cornered animal, he was looking for an escape route.

"I've had dealings with the Russian mob," I said. "They get pretty pissed when things don't go their way. My guess is they're not gonna be too happy that their little scheme got derailed just because you couldn't do your job. You ever see what they do to people who fail them? Believe me, it's not a pretty sight."

Some of the color came back into his cheeks, and his gaze steadied on me.

"Who said their plan's failed?" Had I missed something? The son of a bitch was actually smiling. He took another puff on his cigar. "If you've dealt with the Russians like you said, you must know they always have a backup plan."

True. A lot of the Russian gangsters are former KGB and GRU, people who ran complex espionage and military operations. They would, of course, have contingency plans, and apparently Holiday knew about them.

"So, they have someone other than you and Cora Gables here in Lakeview," I said. "Makes sense. I don't suppose I could get you to tell me who that is?"

"You're a funny man," he said. He laughed and took a sip of his whiskey. "I told you and that cop friend of yours not to stick your nose in my town's business. You should've listened. Now, I'm gonna have to run you out of town."

"You think you'll be able to do that when I tell people you're in bed with the Russian mob?"

"I know I will. This town's mine, Pennyback. I'm a hometown boy, and my dad was chief of police for decades. It'll be my word against yours, an outsider. No, when I get through talking to the city attorney and a few . . . friends on the town council, you and your friend will be about as welcome here as ants at a picnic."

"Even when they learn about the emails you've been getting from your Russian bosses."

A flicker of doubt crept back into his eyes.

"Emails, what emails are you talking about?"

"For starters, the ones ordering you to take care of the mole the Russians inserted into Robert Campbell's restaurant. Oh, by the way, did you know that the Italians knew about her? Looks like they might have been trying to buy her off and maybe that failed and they killed her. Bet the Russians won't be happy to hear that little piece of news."

The flicker of doubt turned to fear. He moved away from the edge of the patio, easing toward the ice chest.

"Italians, what Italians you talking about?"

Now, he was just making idle conversation. He *knew* what Italians. He looked quickly down toward the ice chest.

"I'm talking about the Mafia, Holiday," I said. "The people who're using Gavin Laine's restaurant for all who knows what. Don't tell me you didn't know about that."

He laughed harshly. "Gavin Laine's nothing but trailer trash. That operation he's running for the Eye-ties is peanuts. Now, Ivan, he knows how to make money. Pretty soon, old Gavin and his goombas will be history."

He was pretty close to the ice chest now, and I got an itchy feeling; the kind I used to get just before the shooting started. I took two steps left and put my foot on the lid of the ice chest.

"Don't even think about it," I said.

He took a step back.

"Doesn't matter. It's still your word against mine, and in this town, your word ain't worth a lump of dog shit."

The sound of tires screeching on a hard surface at the front of the house caused us both to turn our heads.

"How about your own words, though? You gonna call yourself a liar?"

"What're you talkin' about?" He backed up another two steps, again at the edge of the patio.

Just then, Williams and Lewis, their guns drawn, came around the corner of the house followed by a grinning Buster.

"Did you get it all?" I asked.

Williams held up his left thumb. "Clear as

a bell, Al," he said.

Holiday's eyes went wide and his mouth flopped open and shut. "Wha-, you son of a bitch, you wearing a wire?"

I unbuttoned the top two buttons of my shirt and showed him the button mike taped to my chest.

"That's right, chief," Williams said. "And, we got it all on tape."

He and Lewis, their weapons held loosely and aimed at the ground, advanced on their boss, who stood quivering at the edge of the patio. He looked from them to me, anger and panic warring for space on his face.

Then, his hands relaxed. The cigar fell and bounced off the stones into the grass. The glass exploded into several pieces and the remains of his drink seeped into the crevices between the stones. And then, he did the dumbest thing.

Why people, when confronted by the authorities, caught dead to rights, and with no place, really, to go, decide to run, is beyond me, and when they're as overweight and out of shape as Samuel Holiday, it's just plain stupid. But, that's what he did.

After dropping the glass and cigar, he bolted for the corner of the building away from his approaching police officers, his shoes making slapping sounds on the stone patio.

"Stop," Lewis yelled.

The two cops began to pursue.

I watched Holiday pumping his arms and legs as he fled toward the corner. When he was still ten feet from making the turn, I leaned over, picked up the half-full whiskey bottle, cocked it behind my ear, and let fly, bottom first.

The bottle flew in an almost perfect spiral in a gentle arc and the bottom caught him at the base of his skull, making a little slapping sound. His arms flew out to his sides, and he pitched forward, making an 'oomph' sound as he hit the grass.

Williams and Lewis were standing over his prostrate form within seconds, holstering their weapons and reaching for their handcuffs. They both had triumphant smiles on their faces.

"Good throw," Buster said, sidling up beside me. "Man, that's gotta hurt, though."

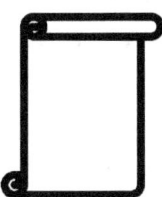

TWENTY-NINE

With Holiday, conscious and cursing up a blue streak, handcuffed in the rear of their cruiser, Williams and Lewis, their faces lit up in broad smiles, stood at the front of the car, facing Buster and me.

"I guess we need to call the state police and the feds right away," Williams said. "Man, this is gonna cause a shit storm; the chief of police being involved with the Russian mob."

"Before you call anyone, could you hold off a few hours," I said.

"Why?"

"We still have one more piece of trash to pick up."

They were already pumped up over arresting their own chief—probably seeing commendations in their futures—but, when I told them what I wanted to do next, they jumped up and down and high-fived each other like high school athletes who just won a state championship.

"You mean this guy Laine's actually tied in with the Mafia?" Lewis said. His face was red with excitement.

'No doubt in my mind," I said.

"We gonna swoop in and arrest him?" Williams asked.

Buster stood quietly by, looking at them with an enigmatic smile on his face.

"Whoa, lads," I said. "It's not that easy. Laine has a video monitoring system, and from what I can tell, he spends a lot of time in his office watching it. We bust in like gangbusters, and he's out the back door and in the wind.."

"So, how do we take him?" Lewis asked. "You want one of us to go around back. I vote Derwood for that job."

"Oh, no you don't, I'm going in the front. You can take the back."

They fairly quivered with excitement. I suppose I was once that young and full of piss and vinegar, but that was a long time ago. Buster, too, looked at them with a fatherly smile, no doubt remembering his own rookie days on the DC force.

"I think we can all go through the front," I said. "Just not together." Their excited looks turned to confusion. "I'll go in first. I've been here before, so that's not likely to alarm anyone. Give me three minutes. I'll distract the goons somehow. You swoop in and arrest 'em, and I'll dash into the back and grab Laine before he can take a powder."

"You sure you'll have time to do that?" Buster asked.

It was taking a chance, I knew. But, I remembered that Laine's office was at the end of the hallway, and the fire exit door was in the middle of that hallway. He would have to run toward the door from the dining area, so if we were able to get the goons under control quickly enough, I had a chance of intercepting him. The smart thing, I know, would have been to cover the back, but Williams and Lewis were like kids at their first Christmas. I wanted both of them to be able to say they went in through the front door and busted up a gangland infiltration of their town. Besides, if Laine did manage to elude me, it would only be temporary. Fleeing would be an admission of guilt, and he would have every law enforcement officer in upstate New York looking for him.

"Yeah, I'll have time. Give me three minutes, and then come in hot," I said.

"Just remember," Buster said. "These

guys are likely to be packing, so keep your wits about you."

"From the bulges in their clothing I saw when I was there before, they *are* armed, so be careful."

Both of them nodded, but from the excited looks on their faces, I wasn't sure they were really hearing me. I gave Buster a look. He'd have to watch over them. He nodded. He's been down that road before. Rookie cops going on their first big bust, sometimes get so excited they aren't as careful as they should be. When the adrenalin gets to pumping, it can affect reason. I saw the same thing with young soldiers going into combat for the first time. It's the job of veterans like Al and me to keep them safe until they get seasoned.

"Say, what do we do with the chief while we go after this guy?" Williams asked.

That was a good sign. He was still thinking in a reasonably rational manner.

"We'll let my partner watch him until we wrap Laine up, and then we'll take both of them in at the same time. That ought to look good on the evening news."

That was sure to turn more than a few heads in city government.

We drove back to the hotel, and deposited Holiday in Heather's room. I instructed her to bash his head with one of the heavy crystal ashtrays if he tried anything. She made him sit on the floor in the corner of her room near the balcony, and put the ashtray on the edge of the desk near her laptop. The look she gave him convinced me that she would do exactly what I'd instructed. It must have convinced him, too. He just sat wedged in the corner, glaring at her.

They parked the police car just outside the Rizzoli parking lot, and we approached the restaurant on foot.

I stopped them at the door. "Okay," I said. "I'll go in first. Give me three minutes to distract his goons if they're there, and then come in and take 'em."

With a last look at Buster who nodded, I opened the door and entered the restaurant. It took a few seconds for my eyes to adjust to the dim interior after the brightness outside. The sleazy little guy sitting behind the plants to right of the door stepped in front of me as I started to go past him, and raised a hand as if to stop me. I gave him my 'angry black man you don't want to mess with' look, and he quickly stepped back behind the plants.

The two goons were still holding up the end of the bar. Their heads swiveled my way as I crossed the room, and their expressions were not welcoming.

I ignored them and turned slightly right, aiming for the door to the right of the bar. They rose from their stools and moved to intercept me. I beat them to the door, stopped and turned.

"You can't go in there," the nearest one said. His breath smelled like dirty gym socks and he had gap between his two front teeth.

"I need to see Laine."

"Well, he don't wanna see you," the other one, slightly bigger with a bump on his nose, looking like it had been broken and not set properly.

I moved to get them to face me, with their backs to the door.

"I'm pretty sure he'll want to see me. I have some information for him."

"Whyn't you tell me, and I'll pass it to him," gap tooth said.

Buster, followed by the two young cops, entered the restaurant. The sleazy lurker started from behind the plants, but Buster put a finger to his lips and scowled at him. He disappeared even faster than he'd done for me. The three of them started making their way quietly across the room.

"Sorry, friend," I said. "But, this is for his ears only."

Gap tooth started forward. "I'll go ask him if he wanna talk to you."

I felt a moment of panic. I needed them both to stay together with their backs to the room. I also needed Buster to hurry our two rookies along before Laine spotted them and ran. Then, someone bumped a chair. Bump Nose looked over his shoulder. When he saw Buster and two cops in uniform, his mouth flew open. "Shit, Guido, cops," he said, and started reaching into the ill-fitting jacket he wore, and turning.

Gap tooth also reached inside his jacket and started turning.

Buster and the cops were still too far away. If these two got their guns out, there would be a fight, and there were five people in waiters uniforms scattered about the place, two women and three men. There was too much chance of collateral damage.

In a split second, I made a decision and took action. Thrusting both hands forward, thumbs spread and to the inside. I slammed by hand into their throats, hitting right on the bumps in their necks with the junction of thumb and forefinger. I hit hard enough to severely bruise, but not enough—I hoped—to break their larynxes. Their guns were forgotten as their hands flew to their damaged throats. They made gurgling sounds and their eyes bulged out of the sockets as they sank to their knees.

They were still gasping for breath when Williams and Lewis came up behind them, each of them grabbing a goon's hands and pulling them roughly behind their backs. After cuffing them securely, large, deadly-looking .45 caliber automatics were removed from the holsters they wore under their jackets.

"Shoot," Lewis said. "You didn't really need us here to do anything but put the cuffs on."

I didn't wait around to make an apology, I yanked open the door and stepped into the hallway.

Laine, carrying a bulging gym bag slung over his left shoulder that slowed him a bit, was jogging toward the fire exit door. I was ten feet away from it; he was about eight and closing. When he saw me, he pumped his legs harder.

I shoved off using the door frame as a launch pad. It was really no contest. I do a lot of running. I was never a short distance runner, preferring distances over two miles, but I can do the hundred yard dash in less than ten seconds, which isn't shabby. And, I didn't have a heavy gym bag slowing me down. We arrived at the fire exit door at the same time.

As he reached for the cross bar to push the door open, I grabbed the gym bag strap and pulled him toward me. He 'yipped', and tried slipping the bag off his shoulder, but I'd reeled him close enough to be able to get my other hand bunched in the collar of his coat.

"Going somewhere, friend?" I said.

"P-please, let me go," he said. "I gotta get out of here. You can have what's in the bag if you let me go."

"Now, you know I can't do that. Besides, you go out that door, and every cop between Canada and the Mexican border will be looking for you."

He was trembling like a willow tree in a stiff breeze, and his face was covered in sweat. "I'll take my chances with the cops.

It's Dominic Vitelli I'm worried about."

"Who is Dominic Vitelli?"

"He's the guy I answer to . . . the person who bankrolled me in this restaurant. When he finds out we've been busted, he's likely to put out a contract on me."

"This Vitelli sounds like a real piece of work." I thought he might be embellishing the story a bit. While the mob can be vicious, that sounded like extreme punishment for a situation over which Laine had no control. "But, do you think he'd really kill you just because this operation's exposed."

"You don't know Dominic," he said. He was breathing so hard, I was afraid he'd hyperventilate and pass out on me. He was wavering on his feet. "I heard a rumor that he killed one of his soldiers for being late picking up money from one of his loan sharking operations. He's one of the lower bosses in the New York organization, and he's trying to move up. Setting up shop here was a long shot, and if it fails, he fails. Dominic doesn't take failure too well."

I sympathized with him. Though not quite to the point of murder, I'd worked with bureaucrats like this Vitelli character, people who were scratching and clawing their way up the organizational ladder, and leaving a lot of bodies—metaphorically—in their wake. Unfortunately for him, my sympathy didn't extend to letting him go.

"Well, if you're willing to tell the

authorities what you know, maybe they can put you in witness protection."

"B-but, that would mean leaving here, all my friends—"

"Would you rather be dead?"

He closed his eyes and furrowed his brow. I could not believe it; the guy was actually *thinking* about it. He must have been making a lot of money from the operation to do that. Finally, though, good sense prevailed.

"Okay, I'll talk."

He sagged in my grip. I slung the gym bag over my left shoulder and grasped his shoulder with my right hand, propelling him toward the dining area.

The two goons had partially recovered from my little love taps. They were sitting at a nearby table, their arms handcuffed behind their backs, glaring murderously at Buster and the two smiling cops. Heads turned our way when we walked through the door.

"You got him," Williams said.

"Yeah." I held up the gym bag. "He was trying to scarper with what feels like a lot of money. He's willing to give us the goods on his mob bosses."

Gap Tooth looked up at Laine, his beetle brow furrowed and his eye brows almost meeting over the bridge of his nose like to dark caterpillars kissing. "You do that, Laine, and you're a dead man," he said.

Laine shrank back against me. "He's lying," he said. "I never said any such thing.

Officers, this man assaulted me, and I want to press charges."

I tightened my grip on his collar. "What about what you just told me," I said. "About this guy, Dominic Vitelli?"

"I d-don't know what you're talking about. I have no idea how you even know that name."

"Why, you lying little weasel." I dropped the gym bag and cocked my left fist back behind my ear.

"That's okay, Al," Williams said. "If he told you anything, we got it on tape."

"Huh?"

He laughed.

"You're still wearing the wire, remember," he said. "I turned the recorder on when we got out of the car. Every conversation you've had has been recorded."

Laine paled. I spun him around and pulled him up so my face was an inch from his. Sweat was pouring off his face and his entire body was quivering. "Witness protection sounds pretty good right now, doesn't it?"

He fainted.

"Might as well cuff him before he comes to and changes his mind again," I said to Williams. "Oh, and we need to consider editing that wire recording. I'm not sure anyone else needs to hear my instructions to Heather about your boss."

The two young cops laughed. "You

kidding," Williams said. "The guys at headquarters will get a kick out of it, and I'm pretty sure the city attorney will want a personal copy. Chief Holiday isn't exactly his favorite person."

"Yeah, but the feds . . ."

He winked. "Well, of course, we'll give them a clean copy."

I was really beginning to like this kid.

I looked around. We had three handcuffed suspects in the restaurant and another in Heather's hotel room. It wouldn't do for either Buster or me to use our cars for transport.

"I think you'd better call for some additional prisoner transport," I said.

"You're right, and I know just who to call," he said, smiling. "She's been drafted as the chief's personal driver so much, I'm pretty sure she'll enjoy the hell out of giving him this one last ride."

I pictured the hefty cop who'd been sitting scowling behind the wheel when Holiday paid his first visit to me. So, it hadn't been me she was scowling at after all.

THIRTY

Four police cars showed up, the entire Lakeview police department, minus the dispatcher and the two crime scene technicians, to transport our prisoners to the town lockup. The smiles as Samuel Holiday was ushered into the back seat of the vehicle he'd been previously chauffeured around in would have lit up a dozen Christmas trees. A ruddy faced redhead with sergeant's stripes on his uniform assumed control as acting police chief, and just before leaving, thanked Buster and me for cracking what was the biggest crime in Lakeview in his fifteen years on the force.

I should have been happy, but I wasn't. I still hadn't solved the crime that started the whole thing. I didn't know who had killed Vivienne LeClerc/Cora Lee Gables.

"Man, this is one vacation I'm not forgetting in a while," Buster said.

He, Heather and I were standing outside the entrance to the spa watching the procession of police vehicles, their red and blue lights flashing, leave the area enroute to Lakeview's town center.

"You can say that again," Heather said.

"It's not over yet, guys," I said.

Heather looked up at me, frowning.

"Wha-, the restaurant's open and seems to be doing well, and we just broke up two criminal gangs that could have led to open warfare between the Russians and the Mafia," she said. "How can you say it's not over?"

"We still haven't found Cora Gables' killer."

"Shit," Buster said. "And, you're not leaving 'till you do, right?"

"We've hit a dead end on that one," Heather said.

"Maybe, maybe not," I said. "What we do know is that it wasn't her Russian bosses and not likely the Mafia who did it . . . not their M.O., so that leaves one of the people who work at the restaurant."

"Are you ruling out a completely unknown person doing it?" Buster asked.

I thought about that for a few seconds. It couldn't be ruled out *completely*, but it didn't feel right. "What are the chances, someone not from here would be able to get into that restaurant at night and get her in the freezer?" They both shook their heads. "No, it had to be someone who knew the place, and knew her habits."

"Muncie," Buster said.

"Maybe, but he's too easy."

"So, what do we do?"

"Two things," I said. "Heather, go back over every one of them with a fine tooth comb. We're missing something. Buster, you and I are going to talk to each one of them again, only this time, we're boring into their souls. One of those people killed Cora Gables, and we're gonna find out which one."

They gave me that resigned look, the expression you see on the face of a father after a roller coaster ride with his kid, and the kid wants to go again. He really doesn't want to do it, but can't say no to the kid. That's what they were, reluctant passengers on my wild ride as I rode off to, probably in their opinion, joust with windmills.

Charles Ray

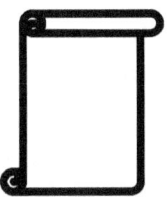

THIRTY-ONE

Buster and I left Heather in her room hunched over her laptop, oblivious to anything but the colorful images on its screen, and walked to Fantastic Fusions.

We found everyone at work except the accountant. I asked Campbell to call him and ask him to drop in for a chat. He looked at me with a querulous expression, but when Buster nodded, he complied. After hanging up the phone, he informed us that Jefferson Aldercott would arrive in an hour, which was fine with me, as it would give us time to question each of those already present.

Campbell graciously gave us the use of his office for the interviews. I wrote the order that I wanted to speak to people on a slip of note paper and asked him to start sending them in.

While we waited for the first subject to arrive, Buster and I rearranged the office. I took Campbell's executive chair from behind the desk and put it in front, facing the door. Then we placed two chairs, back to the door, facing the big chair.

First on our list was Walter Muncie. He wore black pants, a white jacket, and a chef's hat. Dark circles under his bleary eyes indicated lack of sleep. When he entered and I pointed at the big chair facing the door, he looked surprised and a bit wary.

We let him sit and stew for a full minute. He twirled his thumbs, tapped his feet and squirmed in the chair. Finally, he let out a gust of breath.

"What do you want from me? I've got to get ready for the next rush of people. We're expecting a full house, and the guy Mr. Campbell hired to help me is almost useless."

"Just a few questions, Walter, we'll have you back in your kitchen in no time," I said.

Buster leaned forward, a scowl on his face. "But, you gotta tell us the truth this time."

Muncie jerked backwards as if he'd been hit. We hadn't discussed using a good-cop, bad-cop routine, but I trusted Buster's instincts on this. After all, he'd had a lot more experience conducting interrogations than I had.

"Go easy on the kid, Buster, he's overworked, and probably underpaid," I said.

Muncie visibly relaxed and looked at me with a hopeful expression.

"Yeah, besides, I already told you everything I know," he said.

"We just want to double check, Walter," I said. "Now, let's go back to the night Vivienne LeClerc, whose real name by the way was Cora Gables, died. Walk us through it as well as you can remember, minute by minute."

He scratched a stray lock of hair that peeped from underneath the hat. "Well . . . we left you guys at the restaurant . . . I don't remember the exact time." He held both wrists up. "I don't wear a watch, because it gets in the way in the kitchen."

"That's okay. I remember what time it was when you left. What happened next?"

"We walked back here to the restaurant, and went to the kitchen. She went over the menu for the opening with me . . . and told me what she wanted me to do, then, she told me to go home and get some sleep."

"How long were you here?" Buster asked.

"An hour, hour and a half tops."

"What was Cora doing when you left?"

"She was sitting at the big prep table reading the menu for the opening."

A thought occurred to me. I interrupted Buster's questions. "When you arrived, was the building locked?" I asked.

"Uh . . . no, the front door was unlocked. I

remember because I was reaching for my key when Vivienne, er, Cora, just grabbed the handle and opened it."

"Isn't the door locked when there's no one here?"

"It's supposed to be."

"Did you see *anyone* else when you came in?"

"No, but we went straight through to the kitchen. I suppose there could have been someone in the bar area, but I didn't pay any attention. Vi-, er Cora was talking to me at the time."

"Okay, Walter, next question's a sensitive one, but you really need to think about it and answer honestly, okay?"

He rubbed at his eyes. "Sure, I'll answer honestly."

Other than the normal nervousness you'd expect of someone being interrogated, I didn't see any evidence of intent to lie or evade.

"How did you and Cora *really* get along?"

His foot stopped its up and down tapping, and he looked straight into my eyes, but for a fraction of a second, his gaze darted right and up before settling back on its laser focus on me.

"Uh, she was a task master, just like I already told you. Always wanted things done just so . . . and, she had a sort of mean mouth when things didn't . . . go her way."

His voice trailed off. I sensed there was more that he wanted to say.

Buster snarled and started to say something, but I laid a hand on his arm, stopping him.

"There's something else, Walter," I said. "Something you seem hesitant to say. It could be important, though, so please tell us."

He rubbed at his chin, and took a few deep breaths.

"Uh, okay. I know this is gonna sound like I'm trashing the woman now that she's dead, but I'm not. But, I think she was just a big poser, you know. I mean, you already said she wasn't even using her right name, right?"

I leaned forward. "You mean, you suspected that she wasn't who she claimed to be? Why didn't you tell Mr. Campbell?"

He blinked and his cheeks turned red.

"Look, I'm j-just a kid that grew up in Lakeview. I come from the wrong side of t-town. I'm lucky somebody like Mr. Campbell even give me a j-job in the first place. I wasn't about to g-go to him and tell him he got gypped, and his head chef's a f-fraud."

"What made you think she was a fraud, Walter?"

"She was always reading a recipe book," he said. "When I went to cooking school the chefs who taught us hardly ever read a cookbook. They had their signature dishes committed to memory, you know, but she was always consulting a book. The other thing . . . she didn't seem to know a lot about cooking. One time, I told her I was gonna prepare a dish *au* jus and she looked blank at me like she didn't understand what I was saying. Hell, you learn stuff like that the first day in cooking school."

It also meant, though Muncie didn't seem to have recognized it, that her French accent was just for show, too, if she didn't know a common French cooking term.

"I'd think your boss would appreciate knowing that he was being conned," I said.

"That's because you don't understand how things work here in Lakeview," he countered. "Mr. Campbell, he's a lot better than most of the rich folks around here, but in the end, he's still one of them. If you're not one of them, if you're trailer park trash like me, you keep your mouth shut and do what you're told. If I'd gone to him and told him I thought she was a fake, He'd of thought I was just after her job."

"Weren't you?" Buster asked.

"Huh, wasn't I what?"

"Weren't you after her job?" Buster glared at him.

To his credit, other than flinching a bit at Buster's harsh tone of voice, Muncie held gaze with him. "If you mean, did I want her job . . . damn right I did. But, Mr. Campbell had gone and hired himself a fancy French chef. No way was I gonna be able to compete with that. I figured, though, sooner or later, she'd screw up. Like I said, she was a fake. If that woman, Vivienne or Cora, or whatever her name was, was a cook, then I'm a Willow Grove millionaire."

"So," Buster said. "You were just gonna bide your time and wait for her to fuck up."

Muncie's head bobbed up and down. "Why not? My salary as a sous chef's not too bad, and this is my home town. I figured, pretty soon, Mr. Campbell's gonna see she's not as good as she claims, and then he'll can her ass."

"But, he just made you head chef on a temporary basis. He's already talking about hiring someone else to replace her."

"Hey, it was worth a shot. I can at least brag about being head chef for a while. And, who knows, maybe he'll change his mind. Like I said, he ain't quite like the other rich folk around here."

At that point I was almost ready to cross Muncie off the suspect list. He was a lot of things; sneaky and opportunistic came to mind; but, he didn't strike me as a murderer. I wasn't totally eliminating him, though. I've known people to kill for a lot less than a promotion.

"Okay, Walter," I said. "Thanks for your time. You can go back to work now."

Buster sent a questioning look my way. I moved my head from side to side in a negative gesture. He arched his brows as if to say, 'you're kidding, right?', and I just repeated the subtle head shake. Now was not the time to debate the case.

Muncie stood, brushed off his slacks, and left. As he went through the door, Robert Campbell stuck his head in.

"Hey, guys, Jefferson Aldercott's here early. He says he has some important business, and wants to know if you could talk to him right away."

THIRTY-TWO

The first thing I noticed about Aldercott when he walked through the door was that he was nervous. His brown suit was rumpled, and he had a line of sweat above his upper lip. Just as he was taking his seat in the big executive chair, my cell phone rang. I excused myself and went outside to take the call. It was Heather.

"What's up?" I asked.

"Sorry to interrupt you," she said. "But, I just found some information I thought might be useful for you as you ask questions."

She then told me what she'd found. It wouldn't help me learn who'd killed Cora Gables, but it was useful, and timely. I walked back into the office, nodded at Buster and took my chair.

Aldercott was sitting on the edge of the chair, his short legs so short his feet barely reached the floor. He was staring from Buster to me and clutching a battered black soft-sided attaché case. I just stared back at him. His florid cheeks were now glistening with sweat. Buster took his cue from me, and just looked idly at him, his expression neutral.

Finally, Aldercott broke the silence.

"You gentlemen mind telling me why you have me back here? I already told you, I didn't know Ms. LeClerc that well."

I let the silence linger until his eyes were doing a little side-to-side dance as he glanced from me to Buster and back again.

"Actually, Mr. Aldercott," I said. "I think you're lying. I think you know exactly who she was."

He flinched. His eye dance stopped, focusing on a point just below my chin. He was about to tell a lie. You see, a lot of people think that when someone's about to tell a lie, they'll refuse to look at you. In fact, the worse, or best depending upon your point of view, will force themselves to look directly at you in an effort to look like they're being truthful. When they're only so-so, they don't quite make direct eye contact. Aldercott was only so-so. The sweat was now all over his face, and faint half-moons of darkness began appearing at the armpits of his jacket.

"I-I told you before, I knew her name, met her maybe once, but t-that's all."

"You do the payroll records for the restaurant, right?"

"Well, of course. That's part of my contract with Robert."

"Which means you handle the paperwork for the FICA deductions." The Federal Insurance Contribution Act, or FICA deductions, are taken from an employee's pay to cover Social Security and Medicare withholding.

"Sure, I do that paperwork as part of accounting for salaries," he said.

"And, you never noticed that there has never been a Social Security Number issued to Vivienne LeClerc?"

His mouth fell open. A sound like, 'urgh,' came out. Then, he snapped it shut.

"What's the matter," Buster said. "Cat got your tongue."

"Or," I said. "Is it because you *knew* that Vivienne LeClerc was actually Cora Lee Gables, and you were faking the paperwork so that Campbell wouldn't find out?"

"Where are you getting such drivel? I did no such thing." He tried to bluff it, but the tremor in his voice gave him away.

"You're a freelance accountant, right?" I asked.

"Well, yes. I do the books for small firms that don't want to hire a full time accountant."

"You're the accountant for Rizzoli's, the Italian restaurant, and Fantastic Fusions main competitor?"

"Ah, uh, er . . . yes, I do their books, too."

"You don't think there might be a bit of conflict of interest there?"

The way he blinked, I don't think he thought that was the question I was going to ask. Actually, it wasn't, but I wanted to throw him off guard.

"Not really," he said. "I just crunch the numbers they give me. Where's the conflict there?"

His face had started to relax. He was still sweating, though, and I was just about to turn up the heat.

:Well, since you're helping Rizzoli's launder mob money, I figure you'd made the same deal with the Russians for here—through Cora Gables, that is."

Relaxation took a U-turn to make way for panic. His sweat glands started pumping overtime, and his shiny skin was waxy pale. His eyes bugged a bit, and then sort of rolled up in the sockets. He looked like he was about to have a heart attack.

"I d-don't know what you're t-talking about," he said. He licked his lips.

"You probably haven't heard, but the cops just arrested Gavin Laine, and he had a bag full of cash when they busted him. I imagine right about now, he's ratting out everyone involved in the operation to save his own hide, don't you think?"

"Gavin . . . arrested . . . how?"

"Oh, right after they put the cuffs on Police Chief Holiday, they went after Laine. Got him and the two gunsels who hang out at the bar." He was beginning to hyperventilate. "Oh, yeah, forgot to mention, got Holiday on tape admitting that the Russians were planning to use this place as a base of operations to compete with the Italians. That's what I meant about conflict of interest. Don't you think the Italians might object if they found out you were also working for the competition?"

"Chief Holiday, too . . . oh my," he said weakly. "I think I need a lawyer."

Charles Ray

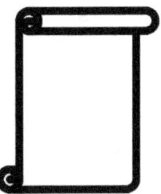

THIRTY-THREE

After that, Aldercott deflated like a tire that's just run over a six-inch nail. He waited, sitting quietly on the edge of the chair, while we called Williams and Lewis to inform that the accountant for the mob operations in Lakeview was sitting with us in the office waiting to be arrested, and, oh by the way, would probably be asking for witness protection. The whoops and cheers on their end of the line were loud enough for Buster to hear sitting three feet away from me. Campbell was crestfallen at the thought of losing his accountant. Aldercott, though, despite being a crook who was playing competing criminal syndicates against each other—and, probably enriching himself in the process—took pride in his profession. He prevailed upon Williams to take his cuffs off long enough to allow him to give Campbell the name and number of an accountant in Mayville who would be able to seamlessly pick up the accounting tasks.

You gotta love small towns. Even when there's been a murder, people still take time to relate to each other.

We called Sunyi Kim in as soon as they'd hauled Aldercott away.

Her interview didn't last long. She repeated pretty much the same thing she'd previously told us, with the exception of adding that she and Jerome Collins had left at the same time, leaving Sanjay Guptar to finish cleaning some metal plates, the kind used under the regular plates at formal dinners, he was working on. When I asked why she and Collins left together, she blushed and said it just happened that they finished what they were working on at the same time, and Guptar, being older and first hired was sort of their unofficial supervisor, had told them to knock off and go home.

I thanked her and sent her on her way.

Next up was Jerome Collins, who came in looking dapper in his waiter's uniform, black pants with a thin red stripe up the side, and a gold-embroidered vest over a pearl colored shirt. When he saw the setup, with the big chair against the desk, and hemmed in by two facing chairs, he frowned.

"What's up, guys?"

I pointed at the big chair.

"Have a seat, Jerome."

Buster just scowled at him.

He started to look worried.

"What's wrong?"

"That depends, Jerome," I said. "On whether or not you're prepared to be honest with us."

"Hey, I already told you what I know. I didn't know Vivienne LeClerc all that well. I mean, she didn't treat me any different than she did anybody else here, but she didn't go out of her way to be friendly either."

"You never suspected that she might not be French?"

"Huh?"

He looked genuinely confused, which I suppose is normal. I threw the question in from left field with the intent of confusing him. I wanted his mind so unsettled he wouldn't have time to make a story up.

"When you left here the night of the . . . incident, was there anyone still here?"

"Sanjay was at the bar polishing them little plate things. He told us, me, to go on home, and he'd lock up."

"You said 'us,' do you mean you and Ms. Kim?"

He looked down at his highly polished

black shoes.

"Uh, yeah, he told the both of us to go home."

"And, you left together?"

There was something like panic in his eyes, and big beads of sweat popped out on his broad, brown forehead.

"Come on, kid," Buster said. "What you holdin' back?"

He wiped at the sweat on his brow, smearing it across his dark skin. Finally, he looked at me with a pleading expression. "Okay, I'll tell you, but you gotta promise me that what I say stays between us."

"I can't really make a promise like that," I said. "It all depends on what you tell me."

"If you haven't broken any law, we can probably keep mum," Buster said. "Have you broken any laws?"

"Oh no, I never even got a parking ticket. It's just . . . well, if it got out, somebody I care a lot about could get in trouble."

"Has this someone broken the law?" I asked.

He shook his head. "No, it's not like that. Okay, I'm gonna trust you guys." He mopped his brow again. "It's Sunyi. Me and her . . . we, er, been seeing each other."

Buster put his hands together and bumped the pads together. He had a big smile on his face. "You mean as in *seeing* each other?"

"No, I mean, yeah, but it's not what you're

thinking. We're in love, see, but her mother's a real hard-nosed Korean. She don't like Sunyi gettin' involved with a non-Korean, and if she knew she was seein' a black dude, she'd pop a blood vessel, so we keep it on the down-low."

"I thought she was from out of state," I said.

"She is, but there's one or two Korean families here in Lakeview, and Sunyi's scared they're in touch with her folks. If they knew she was spendin' nights at my crib, she thinks they'd call her old lady. Man, if they did that, the shit would hit the fan. They'd make here quit her job and come back home."

Buster looked confused, but I was convinced Collins was being truthful. I'd served in Asia enough times when I was in the army to know what the kid was talking about. Asians, especially Asian mothers, are as fiercely protective of their kids as a mama lion, and have claws and fangs just as sharp. Many Asian societies are also, to put it bluntly, very ethnocentric, and view darker races, even darker complexioned people of their own ethnic group, with disdain.

"Okay, Jerome, I believe you. So, just so I'm clear on this; when you and Sunyi left, Guptar was still here?"

"Yeah, he was back by the bar like I said. When we left, he was still sitting there, humming to himself and polishing plates.

Say, you're not gonna repeat what I said about me and Sunyi, are you?"

"Don't worry, kid, your secret's safe with us."

He was smiling when he left.

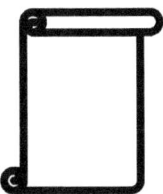

THIRTY-FOUR

When Sanjay Guptar walked into the office, he didn't look nervous, but he did look wary. I eyed him carefully. The way he brushed at imaginary lint on his waiter's jacket. The way he refused to make eye contact. Just as I had a gut feeling that Muncie, despite having motive and possibly opportunity, wasn't the one who'd whapped Cora Gables on the head and left her in the freezer to die, that same gut was telling me that Guptar, for all his wary calm, was hiding something. For one thing, he'd misled me when we first talked. He hadn't made it clear that he didn't leave when Collins and Kim left.

Getting him to talk, though, would require finesse. Well, finesse is my middle name on a good day. On a bad day . . . well, that's another story. Today, though, I'd open with finesse. Besides, Buster, with a brooding look on his face, was there if I needed to move away from finesse.

"Have a seat, Sanjay," I said. "You mind if I call you Sanjay?"

He sat in the big chair, straightening his trouser seams before crossing his legs. "No, I do not mind," he said.

"Good. Thanks for agreeing to talk to us again. I have a few follow-up questions, and I think you can help us clear them up."

"I have already told you everything I can remember, but I am, of course, happy to help further if I am able. What is it that you wish to know?"

What I wished to know was, 'who the hell killed Cora Lee Gables, and why?', to know for sure. I was beginning to get the glimmering of an idea. I just needed to tread carefully to get enough facts to put some substance to it.

"Tell me about the closing procedures here at the restaurant." He looked at me with an expression of bewilderment. "What I mean is, what's the drill, does the last person out lock up or what?"

His expression brightened. "Oh, I see. Yes, that is how we decided to do it. Actually, *I* came up with that idea. The last person to leave in the evening will close and lock the door."

"Interesting," I said. I decided to change the subject. I needed to keep him off balance. But, I was coming back to this issue. Something about it bothered me. "How well did you know the woman known as Vivienne LeClerc?"

"Not very well at all, I'm afraid. She was not, you see, a very easy woman to get to know."

I didn't fail to notice that he didn't react to my offhand comment about LeClerc. I would have expected surprise at a minimum, or a question as to my meaning.

"By that do you mean that she was an unfriendly person?"

He stroked his upper lip and looked up at the ceiling. "Not exactly unfriendly, it was more that she was withdrawn. She did not seem to like engaging with people very much."

"I understand, though, that she was really quite harsh at times with Walter Muncie, her assistant."

"Well, yes . . . she was quite the taskmaster in the kitchen, and, of course, Walter didn't like being referred to as an assistant, even though that is what a sous chef is."

The muscles in his face, tense when he first arrived, were beginning to relax. He uncrossed his legs.

"How did she treat those of you on the wait staff?"

He shrugged. "She was insistent that we respond immediately when an order was announced as ready," he said. "But, other than that, she really had little contact with us."

"One would think . . . in an establishment this small, that there'd be more interaction among the staff."

"We have all been busy preparing for the opening, and have had so many customers since we opened there has been little time for socializing on the job. After work, of course, we each go our separate ways."

He looked to be relaxed enough. I only hoped it was enough for him to be off guard as I moved in to attack.

"Forgive me for asking what might seem an intrusive and personal question, Sanjay, but you're Hindu, right?"

He looked surprised at the question, but only for the briefest of moments. He smiled. "Why yes, I am Hindu. Why do you ask?"

"Is it true that one of your beliefs is that souls are reincarnated, and the status of that reincarnation depends upon how one conducted himself in the present life?"

"Well, that is a bit simplistic, but essentially correct. What does this have to do with Vivienne's death?"

"Well, it just occurred to me that if we were in India, whoever killed her would be worried about his next life right now." I smiled to convey the sense that I was partly joking, but I saw a tiny flicker in his eyes.

"Murder? You are saying that Vivienne was murdered?"

"You know, her name wasn't Vivienne," I said. "In fact, she wasn't even French."

His eyes widened. As an effort to show surprise, though, it was lame, and a bit too late.

"What do you mean? Who was she then?"

I saw no harm at this point in sharing the information with him. Like a lion stalking a gazelle, I had the scent. I was almost ready to pounce.

"Her real name was Cora Lee Gables," I said. "She was a con artist, and it looks like she was working with the Russian mob in an effort to set this restaurant up as a base for their operations in this area."

The surprise on his face was genuine.

"I thought there was something strange about her, but I attributed it to Gallic arrogance. Was she even really a chef?"

"About as much as I am." I laughed, which caused him to flinch. "She had a collection of cookbooks at her place. I think she studied them at night so she could pull off the cook ruse during the day."

He closed his eyes. "That would explain it."

"Explain what?"

"She was always reading." He opened his eyes. "Whenever she was not cooking or chastising Walter, she was hunched in the back of the kitchen, near the spice storage bin, reading."

"I thought you said you didn't know her well."

"Huh?" His dark brown cheeks turned darker.

"For someone you didn't know well, you seem to know a lot about her activities."

"Uh, I just noticed that when I happened to be passing through the kitchen."

His eyes were dark brown, almost black, and they darted quickly from side to side. He probably wasn't even aware of it.

"You said earlier that the last person to leave had to lock the place, right?"

"Yes."

"What did that person do with the key?"

"Oh, that person would take the key home," he said. "He or she would have to come in early the following day and open the door, otherwise, Mr. Campbell would have to come in and open."

"He probably came in early most mornings anyway," Buster said. "The Bob Campbell I remember from school was an early riser."

"Yes, that is so," Guptar said. "Mr. Campbell was often the first to arrive in the mornings."

"Was he the first to arrive the morning LeClerc . . . Gables' body was found?"

"No, he was not here. I unlocked the door."

"So, you had the key. That means you

locked it the night before."

"Uh, yes, I did lock it. I left right after Jerome and Sunyi."

Bingo. I was convinced that Walter Muncie was being truthful when he said the door was unlocked when he and LeClerc/Gables arrived.

"So, you locked up the night before, opened that morning, and it was you who discovered the body."

His gaze locked with mine. His eyes were like two ink dots, completely devoid of life.

"Yes, that is true," he said.

I should have seen it earlier. The first on the scene at most crimes should be looked at as a likely suspect. Arsonists like to look at their handiwork, and murderers will often insert themselves into the investigation, either to keep track of what's going on, or just to gloat. As I looked into his lifeless eyes, I could see that awareness was dawning; he was beginning to realize that I was on to him.

"What happened between you two?"

"I do not understand what you mean?"

But, he did. He was just struggling to maintain the crumbling façade of his innocence.

"I think you do," I said. "I think I can tell you what happened here that night, but I'm having trouble with the why. Help me out, Sanjay. Tell me why you killed her? Was it an accident? A little misunderstanding that got out of hand?"

Was he going to continue to defy me? For a moment it looked like he would. But then, the remaining bricks of the façade crumbled to dust. He slumped in the chair, his chin almost on his chest.

"I did not mean to kill her," he said "It was . . . she just made me so angry."

"What happened?"

He looked at us for a long time. When he began to talk, his body relaxed, and the tension lines in his face melted away.

"I went to her for help," he said. "I was supposed to be the *maître d'* here, but Mr. Campbell was hiring that Bennie Suarez for the job." The dark pools of his eyes were now showing life, the fire of anger blazed. "I am far more qualified. Of course, I could not go directly to Mr. Campbell. That might be seen as a challenge to his authority. But, I figured that Ms. LeClerc, a beautiful French woman, and head chef, might have some influence over him."

He had asked if she would intercede with Campbell on his behalf regarding the *maître d'* position, but instead of showing at least a bit of sympathy, she'd laughed in his face.

"She said that a *maître d'* had to be polite, but in command, and that I was too . . . obsequious, that I did not have the . . . balls for the job. She just stood there laughing at me. I do not remember clearly what happened next, except that I picked up the wooden chopping board that was on a nearby counter and hit her with it. She fell and did not appear to be breathing. I panicked. I rinsed the board in the sink and then put it back on the counter. Then I pulled her body into the freezer, closed it, and left."

"Then, the next morning, under the pretext of checking the supply of ice, you conveniently discover the body."

"Yes, I wanted to check to see if there was anything that would implicate me. There was not, so I opened the freezer and *found* her body." His eyes almost closed, he looked at me through the narrow slit. "How did you know it was me?"

"At first I didn't," I said. "But, little things kept dropping in front of me, and bit by bit, the trail of bread crumbs led to you. First, there was the issue of the locked, or rather unlocked, door. Muncie said it was unlocked when they arrived, and I'm pretty sure he was being truthful about that. You, though, claim to have locked it when you left, and again, I think you were telling the truth. Those two things together, my friend, put you in the restaurant when they arrived."

"If that is so, why did they not see me?"

"You were in the bar area. Unless you were making noise, and polishing flatware's not exactly a noisy job, they might not have noticed you, since they came in and went straight to the kitchen."

"Okay, let us say that I *was* here, how did you go from that to me being a killer?"

"Well, I have to admit, that had me stumped. Muncie had motive. She treated him like shit. He also had opportunity. But, he just didn't register on my bullshit meter. Neither did you at first. Even when the little clues started pointing at you, I had a problem. You had means and opportunity, but I couldn't see the motive. All this shit with organized crime also threw me off scent. Who would have ever thought that a simple refusal to help you would send you into a rage and lead to murder?"

He looked down at his hands resting on his thighs. When he looked back up at me, his eyes glistened. "I do not know what came over me. I truly regret what I have done."

Maybe he did. Who knows what goes through a person's mind at times like that. Are we all capable of such violence when provoked? That wasn't for me to answer, though. I'd set out to find out who killed Cora Gables. In the process, I'd stumbled across other crimes, that would have probably gone unsolved if a Midwestern con woman hadn't been chosen to infiltrate Buster's friend's restaurant, and then been killed in what Guptar's defense attorney would try to portray as a crime of passion. He death had nothing to do with the others, but it was the pebble that started an avalanche uncovering them.

"You know, Sanjay," I said. "That we'll have to turn you in to the authorities."

He looked resigned to that.

"What do you think will happen to me?"

A simple question, but one that I had no useful answer to; he belonged to the criminal justice system now.

"I can't answer that question, Sanjay."

"I am sorry for what I did; you know that, don't you?"

I wanted to tell him to 'tell it to the judge,' but I was always taught never to kick a man when he's down.

"I guess so," I said.

Whether or not a lawyer could use that line with a judge and jury effectively was anyone's guess. It was no longer my problem.

THIRTY-FIVE

Guptar sat motionless in the chair until two officers from the city police department came to collect him, and made no effort to resist when they cuffed him and led him out to their car.

Robert Campbell was devastated. He'd lost his head chef to murder, and now one of his wait staff was being carted off to jail for the crime. He'd made contact with the new accountant, but was still shaking his head in disbelief at the fact that a man he'd known most of his life had played a key role in trying to make his restaurant part of a criminal enterprise. But, with a few words of cheer from Buster, who reminded him that it was like a game when their team was behind by two touchdowns at halftime and they'd been pounded mercilessly by the offensive line, but knew they could come back for the second half, reenergized and determined to win.

As for me, I was just glad this vacation was over. I've had active cases that were less exciting.

We all, kids included, ate breakfast at 7:30 on Friday morning, and by 9:30 had the luggage stowed in the cars and were in a convoy heading south. Since Sandra and I had taken the Adirondack Forest route, we led the four car caravan. I pulled over when we were about halfway through the national forest when Buster, whose car was second in line, flashed his lights. It turned out that the kids had to pee, which meant Buster had to take little Albert in one direction while Alma took Sandra in another off the road into the trees. After the kids had done their business they, of course, had to chase butterflies for a few minutes. Alma fussed, but it was a nice rest stop, and the forest is beautiful and peaceful.

We entered the town of Westover at half past noon, and ten minutes later saw the rusty sign,

I signaled the turn and pulled into the parking lot. The others followed, and we all

got out.

"Why are we stopping here?" Buster asked.

"I don't know about you," I said. "But, my stomach's growling so loud I can hear it over the sound of the car's engine. I figured we could eat a late lunch, and either skip supper or eat light."

"I got no problem with stopping to eat." He pointed at the modest looking building that was Al's Eats. "My question is, why here?"

Sandra got of the passenger side, walked around and linked her arm in mine. "That was my reaction when we stopped her on the way to Lakeview," she said. "But, trust me; the food's not half bad."

I punched him lightly in the shoulder. "It's like a northern version of Mom's," I said.

"They got fried chicken?"

"Yeah, with nice and creamy mashed potatoes."

Alma walked up beside his, each hand handing onto a squirming toddler. "What about children's menu? They have child-sized portions?"

I shrugged. "I'm sure we can get them to make small servings for the children," Sandra said.

Heather and Quincy were silent, just looking around at the pickups and rusty old cars in the parking lot with dismay.

"Let's to inside," I said, and with Sandra clinging to my arm, led our little procession inside.

The same fat guy who'd served Sandra and me was behind the counter. He looked up when we came in and smiled broadly.

"Well, see you folks decided to drop in again," he said. "And, I see you brought your friends. Welcome, make yourself at home."

There were only ten customers, the lunch hour was almost over, so we were able to get two tables shoved together in the right corner near the front. The owner assured us that he had kid-sized servings. I only hoped he meant normal kid and not farm kid-sized servings. I grew up in a rural area, and some of the farm kids I knew could eat more than two men.

We put in our orders, with plenty of input from the owner. He took the order to the kitchen, and while it was being prepared, brought us our drinks, glasses of milk for the kids and a huge pitcher of lemonade for the adults.

"You're the owner of this place?" Buster asked, as he was pouring our lemonade. He nodded. "So, your name's Al?"

"That's right. Actually it's Al, Junior. My dad was Al, Senior, and he owned it before me."

Buster pointed at me. "My friend here's named Al, too."

"Is that so?" the fat man asked, looking down at me. "That stand for Alfred or Albert?"

"Albert," I said.

"Me too, but Albert sounds too snooty, so I'm must Al to everybody."

"I know what you mean."

He was chuckling as he waddled off. We settled quietly into sipping our drinks. Even the twins were well-behaved and quietly sucking their milk through the straws stuck through the plastic caps Al had put over their glasses.

A few minutes later, Al returned with our food. We'd all settled for fried chicken, mashed potatoes, corn on the cob, corn pones and apple pie with ice cream for dessert. True to his claim, he'd prepared two smaller plates for the children, and provided them with plastic utensils. The food looked good, smelled fantastic, and when I took my first bite of a golden brown drumstick, tasted even better than it looked.

For a few minutes the only sound was the contented sighs and the occasional smacking sound.

When we'd made a significant dent in the food, Buster sat back in his chair. "You know, this is a meal that ought to be eaten slowly; I mean, really enjoyed."

I agreed. I stopped eating, wiped my mouth with a paper napkin, and sat back. "You're right. If we were at Mom's she'd be telling us to slow down, the food ain't going nowhere."

"You know, one time, you two are going to have to take me to Mom's," Alma said. "The way you talk about her, I'm starting to get jealous."

Buster spewed lemonade across the table. I was fortunate that my mouth was empty, or I would have done the same.

"Alma, you don't have to worry on that score," I said. "Mom's old enough to be Buster's mother, and she has to weigh three hundred pounds if she's an ounce. She just happens to be the best cook in DC."

"That's for sure," Buster said. "She makes the best soul food south of the Mason-Dixon Line."

"Are you saying there's a better cook *north* of the Mason-Dixon Line?" Sandra asked.

Buster smirked. "No way, ain't no soul food up here. They got good food, but it ain't soul food. Only place you find soul food is in the south."

I've could have argued with him on that point . I've had some great meals of fried chicken, black-eyed peas, and corn fritters in Chicago, and found a couple of nice southern-style restaurants in Oakland, not far from the army terminal, when I deployed through California on my way to the Far East. But, I didn't want to spoil the mood.

"Maybe next weekend, we can take everyone there," I said. Sandra made a face. She's not fond of too much fried food. I patted her hand. "Once a month won't kill you, babe. I think you'll like it, actually."

"Okay, I'll try it once," she said. She took a

sip of lemonade. "So, tell me what you four were up to. I heard gossip around the spa that you not only caught that woman's killer, but some gangsters as well."

Buster, Heather, and I took turns filling her in. When we'd finished, she sat there with tears in her eyes.

"That poor woman, left to die like that," she said. "It's so sad."

Heather reached across the table and patted her wrist. "I looked it up on the Internet," she said. "She actually probably didn't even suffer, especially if she was unconscious."

Sandra's face contorted in shock. Sandra and Heather get along, despite being almost polar opposites; Sandra's athletic, while Heather's more at home at a computer keyboard; Sandra's all emotion, and Heather can sometimes come across like me, pretty coldblooded. I didn't want to see their relationship disrupted over this, though, so I patted Sandra's other wrist.

"Heather's right, you know. Freezing to death is probably the least painful way to go, because you usually fall asleep before you die. Of course, in this case, Guptar had hit her so hard it's unlikely she ever woke up. What's really sad is why he attacked her in the first place."

That distracted her. "And, all because she refused to talk to the boss about promoting him. He sounds like he has some unresolved anger issues to me."

"I should have noticed it when I first met him," I said. "The way he focused on polishing the silver and the tightness in his voice should have alerted me. But, I was so keyed on Muncie as the most likely suspect, I didn't notice."

"Hey, don't beat yourself up, bro," Buster said. "It happens to the best cops sometimes. We get focused on a suspect, and the real perp skates. What turned you in his direction, anyway?"

"Well, it started with the open door. When Muncie said the door was open when they arrived, I sensed that he was telling the truth. That meant someone else was there when they arrived. Collins and Kim also seemed to be telling the truth about leaving before Guptar, a fact that he conveniently neglected to mention when we first talked to him. It was really just a process of elimination. The problem was motive; I couldn't for the life of me figure out his motive for killing her."

Sandra laid her head against my shoulder. The smell of the shampoo she'd used that morning tickled my nose. "Knowing you, though, once you got that lead, you weren't about to quit until you got the answer."

"That was pretty slick, the way you used that Hindu reincarnation stuff on him."

"I wasn't sure it would work," I said. "We got lucky on that. You know, I think he was relieved to get it off his chest."

Little Albert Mayweather, his cherubic brown face dotted with mashed potatoes, pointed across the table at me. "Unka Al got the bad guy."

Sandra Mayweather, her face a lot neater than his, but with flakes of fried chicken on the front of her jumper, was not to be outdone by her brother. She smacked her spoon on the table. "He always get the bad guy, doo doo head!"

Everyone around the table, even Alma who didn't normally allow them to use such language, laughed, sending bits of food spraying across the tablecloth. Heads turned our way, with brows raised. The owner, his beefy arms folded across his flabby chest, smiled and nodded. The raised brows lowered and everyone smiled. Just a large extended family having a nice time over a nice meal, folks; nothing to be worried about. You can't be more normal than that.

Beaming proudly, Buster reached over and patted them both on the head. "That's right, kids," he said. "Your Uncle Al always gets his man." He looked at me and winked. "Even when he's on vacation."

"It would've been nice to get paid for all we did," Heather said.

"Hey, Bob said all of us eat free for life at his place," Buster said.

I looked at Sandra. She shook her head.

"Thank him for me," I said. "But, I'm not

gonna be taking any more vacations any time soon. All I want to do now is get home."

"Wanna go home," the twins sang in unison. "Wanna go home."

From the mouths of babes.

Sandra and I sang along to old songs from the fifties all the way home.

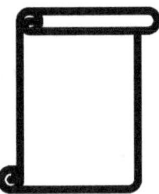

THIRTY-SIX

On Saturday, Sandra and I woke up late, late for us that is, around 7:30. We did our run, martial arts workout, showered, ate a light breakfast, and went back to bed. And, we slept away most of the day, only waking up around 4:30, and after a little bed play, got up and gave the old farm house a good cleaning.

As a result of sleeping in on Saturday, we were refreshed Sunday morning. After working out, showering, and eating a substantial breakfast, we took our second cups of coffee to the back porch where we sat watching a herd of Whitetail deer graze at the edge of the woods behind the house. Two

young bucks, one a four-pointer who looked
to be developing into a strapping alpha male,
and a younger buck whose antlers were just
beginning to develop points, led four does
and two fawns still with the white spots
indicating they were born in late spring, out
of the trees and into the knee-high grass that
I never mowed. The lead buck stopped and
stared in our direction, alert to any sudden
moves on our part that would signal danger.
We left our cups on the folding table between
our chairs and sat as still as we could,
looking back at him. Apparently satisfied that
we weren't predators, he made a 'snuff'
sound and began grazing, raising his head
every few seconds to check us out.

"They are really beautiful animals,"
Sandra said quietly.

"Yeah, as long as you don't get the ticks
that feed on their blood on you," I responded
just as quietly. "Lyme Disease is no joke."

"I don't want to pet them, just look at
them. They're so graceful and peaceful."

"True. Besides, they'd never let you get
close enough to pet." They were accustomed
to our presence on the deck, sometimes
coming within twenty feet or so to graze, but
whenever we moved toward them, they bound
back into the trees, their white tails straight
up in the air.

She reached across the table and pinched
my forearm, not too hard, just enough to let
me know that my nature and health lecture

was not appreciated.

"You can be a real killjoy at time, you know that," she said. "I just mentioned it to say that we don't really need to travel for a vacation. Just sitting here on your back porch observing nature is vacation enough for me."

I reached across and rubbed her hand. "For me too, babe," I said. "Being here with the one I love, enjoying nature and a good cup of coffee relaxes me, and that's what a vacation is supposed to be for after all, right?"

She laid her free hand on mine.

"It was quite a trip, though. Who else but you would run into a murder and organized crime on a vacation?"

I laughed. Not loud enough to startle the deer. "Yeah, that was something. At least, we solved the crime, so it wasn't a total waste."

:"Just think," she said. "If you, Heather, and Buster hadn't been there, not only would the murder have been ruled an accident, but two vicious gangs would have their hooks in that town. It was like fate decreed it."

"Fate, blind luck; whatever you choose to call it, at least we got at the truth.

Her brow wrinkled and she had a worried look in her eyes.

"What's the matter?" I asked.

"I was just wondering. Did you *really* bet the whole truth?"

"Meaning?"

She picked up her cup and took a sip. Then, she carefully and quietly put the cup back on the table.

"I've been thinking about what happened," she said. "You solved that poor woman's murder by process of elimination, right?"

"Well, sure. The other possible suspects either had alibis, or were being truthful when I questioned them."

"And, you still have the ability to tell when someone's lying to you?"

"Of course."

"Then, why were you unable to detect that Sanjay Guptar was lying when you first spoke to him?"

A little bell went off in my head. She was right. When I first spoke to Guptar, I didn't get any indication that he was being evasive or untruthful. It was only after I brought up the reincarnation thing that he'd crumbled.

"Damn," I said. "That's a good point. The only liars I can't read are the ones who are psychopaths, or people who honestly believe they're telling me the truth."

"And, you said that even after he confessed, he didn't seem remorseful, only intrigued that you'd tripped him up."

"Yeah, I figured he was just in shock. I mean, he'd just been caught out as a killer. That's enough to rattle anyone."

"Babe, he slammed a woman's head hard enough to put her in a coma, then he puts the murder weapon back in its proper place in the kitchen, far away from the body, left it in the freezer, and closed the freezer door. Does that sound like someone who rattles easily?"

"Well, according to Collins and Kim, he freaked out when he discovered the body."

"When you talked to him shortly afterwards, did he seemed rattled?"

I replayed that meeting in my mind. No, he wasn't the least bit rattled. In fact, for someone who'd just found a colleague's body in the freezer, he was quite composed.

"Holy shit! I think he played me."

"A good lawyer, though, will use his reaction after finding the body to show his mental state," she said. "But, who kills someone just because they won't help them get a job, and then has the presence of mind to stage the body and move the weapon?"

Shit. With a good lawyer, he'd probably plead to and get convicted of involuntary homicide, or even manslaughter. I wasn't familiar with the way the courts worked in New York, but I could see him getting paroled after a few years in the slammer. Hell, he might even plead temporary insanity and get sent away to some psychiatric institution until he 'recovered.'

Not on my watch. I like solving puzzles, and I *don't* like being played for a patsy. I stood up suddenly, causing my chair to thump against the wood boards of the porch. The deer stopped grazing, their heads up, and a heartbeat later were bounding for the dark recesses of the forest.

"Pack a bag, babe," I said. "We're taking a road trip."

"Will we have time to visit Chautauqua Institute this time? Quincy said it's a really nice place, and I never got to see it except from across the lake."

Author's Note

While the descriptions of the area around Lake Chautauqua in upstate New York are accurate, the town of Lakeview is entirely fictional, as are the establishments mentioned in this story. I've visited this region many times, and I can assure you that I've never encountered any evidence of organized crime activity. It's actually a peaceful, scenic area, and all the people I've met there are warm, welcoming, law-abiding citizens, so I apologize to them for setting this heinous crime in their home area.

Charles Ray

Other books by this author:

Al Pennyback mysteries

Color Me Dead
Memorial to the Dead
Deadline
Dead, White, and Blue
A Good Day to Die
The Day the Music Died
Die, Sinner
Deadly Intentions
Death by Design
Till Death Do Us Part
Deadly Dose
Dead Man's Cove
Dead Men Don't Answer
Deadly Paradise
Kiss of Death
Death in White Satin
Death and Taxis
Deadbeat
A Deadly Wind Blows
Death Wish
Deadly Vendetta
A Time to Kill, A Time to Die
Dead Ringer
Death of Innocence
Dead Reckoning
Murder on the Menu

Ed Lazenby mysteries
Butterfly Effect
Coriolis Effect
The Cat in the Hatbox

The Buffalo Soldier series:
Buffalo Soldier: Trial by Fire
Buffalo Soldier: Homecoming
Buffalo Soldier: Incident at Cactus Junction
Buffalo Soldier: Peacekeepers
Buffalo Soldier: Renegade
Buffalo Soldier: Escort Duty
Buffalo Soldier: Battle at Dead Man's Gulch
Buffalo Soldier: Yosemite
Buffalo Soldier: Comanchero
Buffalo Soldier: Range War
Buffalo Soldier: Mob Justice
Buffalo Soldier: Chasing Ghosts
Buffalo Soldier: The Piano

Other fiction
Angel on His Shoulder
She's No Angel
Child of the Flame
Pip's Revenge
Wallace in Underland
Further Adventures of Wallace in Underland
Dead Letter and Other Tales
The White Dragons

The Dragon's Lair
Dragon Slayer
The Last Gunfighters
The Culling
Frontier Justice: Bass Reeves, Deputy
  U.S. Marshal
Angel on His Shoulder-Revised Edition
Battle at the Galactic Junkyard
Mountain Man
Devil' Lake

Nonfiction
Things I Learned from My Grandmother About
  Leadership and Life
Taking Charge: Effective Leadership for the
  Twenty-first Century
Grab the Brass ring
African Places: A Photographic Journey
  Through Zimbabwe and southern Africa
A Portrait of Africa
There's Always a Plan B
In the Line of Fire: American Diplomats in
  the Trenches
Advice for the Insecure Writer
Looking at Life Through My Lens

Children's books
The Yak and the Yeti
Samantha and the Bully
Molly Learns to Share
Where is Teddy?
Catie and Mister Hop-Hop

About the Author

Charles Ray has been writing fiction since his teens. He won a Sunday school magazine writing contest when he was thirteen, and having his byline on a short story published in a national publication forever hooked him on writing. During his time in the army (1962-1982) he often moonlighted as a newspaper or magazine journalist, and was the editorial cartoonist for the Spring Lake (NC) News, a weekly newspaper, during the 1970s. In addition to his writing, he was an artist/cartoonist and photographer for a number of publications, including Ebony, Eagle and Swan, and Essence, and had a monthly cartoon feature and did several covers for Buffalo, a now-defunct magazine that was dedicated to showcasing the contributions of African-Americans to the country's military history.

After retiring from the army, he joined the U.S. Foreign Service, and served as a diplomat in posts in Asia and Africa until his retirement in 2012. He has worked and traveled throughout the world (Antarctica is the only continent he hasn't visited), and now, as a full time writer, continues to globetrot looking for interesting things to write about, draw, or take pictures of.

A native of Texas, he now calls Maryland

home. For more on his writing and other projects, check one of the following Web sites:

http://charlesaray.blogspot.com
http://charlieray45.wordpress.com
http://www.twitter.com/charlieray45
http://www.facebook.com/charlieray45
http://www.flickr.com/photos/charlesray45/
http://www.viewbug.com/member/charlesray

Author's photograph by Denise Ray-Wickersham

www.ingramcontent.com/pod-product-compliance
Lightning Source LLC
Chambersburg PA
CBHW060357260626
47160CB00006B/2351